# PRETTY WHEN YOU LIE

DARK AND WILD
BOOK ONE

ANNE ROMAN

Copyright © 2023 by ANNE ROMAN

All rights reserved.

No part of this book may be reproduced in any form or by any electronic or mechanical means, including information storage and retrieval systems, without written permission from the author, except for the use of brief quotations in a book review.

This novel is entirely a work of fiction. The names, characters, and incidents portrayed in it are the work of the author's imagination. Any resemblance to actual persons, living or dead, events or localities is entirely coincidental.

Designations used by companies to distinguish their products are often claimed as trademarks. All brand names and product names used in this book and on its cover are trade names, service marks, trademarks, and registered trademarks of their respective owners. The publishers and the book are not associated with any product or vendor mentioned in this book. None of the companies referenced within the book have endorsed the book.

*For my sister, Terran.*
*I'm sorry I didn't name a kid after you. I hope this makes up for it. Please stop bringing it up now.*

PREFACE

I hope you like angst, suspense, and sexy-alpha-hole bikers because this book has it. I also hope you don't hunt me down at the end because that's certainly what a few of my beta readers threatened to do. It's ok though, I still love them. I'm a reader that loves twists, turns, and mic-drop moments that leave your heart racing and your mind going w.t.f. just happened! So there's a lot of that in this book. If you love that, then you'll probably love Pretty When You Lie and the subsequent books to follow. But if you don't...well, don't say I didn't warn you.

**Possible Triggers:**
Dub Con (mild)
Virgin heroine
Graphic sex

PREFACE

Violence/Murder
Emotional abuse
Explicit Language
Revenge Fucking
Spankings
*cough Cliffhanger cough*
Xoxo- Anne

## 1

JUNIPER

The solid oak door slammed shut behind me with a finality that echoed in my soul. I stood on the wrap-around porch of my childhood home, my entire body vibrating with rage and hurt.

He'd gone too far this time.

I heaved giant sobs, my hands shaking with fear. I couldn't stay anymore. Not in that house. Not with that man. The thought of leaving my home caused another sob to rip through me.

But I had to keep reminding myself that it wasn't a home. It was more like a prison.

My father didn't raise his voice when he argued. He didn't yell or scream. He'd just stare at me like a hawk watching his prey, waiting for the opportunity to strike. Waiting for a moment of weakness. And inevitably, the weakness would reveal itself. A question I didn't answer correctly or thought I failed to follow up on. That's what happens when your father is a successful and powerful lawyer to some of the most dangerous criminal organizations in the state. There's no need for theatrics. You just have to ask the right questions, bide your time, and your opponent will open themselves up to your attack. Then it's game over.

Tears threatened to fall down my cheeks, but I refused to let them. Instead, I stormed across the lawn to the circular drive and my sunshine yellow 1969 Volkswagen Beetle. My father had wrinkled his nose in disdain when I'd first pulled up to the house with my prized possession, but he hadn't objected. It was my only freedom. I was surprised he allowed it, considering he carefully planned and controlled every other waking minute of my life. But it was more than just a car to me, it was my lifeline to my mother.

Before she'd gotten sick, my mother would tell me stories about her days traversing all over the countryside in a Volkswagen, just like mine. I'd sat at her bedside and listened to her talk about her adventures as a carefree gypsy, with rapt attention. Where my father was cold and calculated, all business suits and ties, my mother had been flowing dresses with wildflowers from the fields around our city braided in her hair. I'd wanted to believe that they loved each other, although I suspected that wasn't the case. But then my mother had gotten sick shortly after Dean's birth, and my father became a disapproving shadow, ever-present in our house and in my head.

Cranking up the car and pulling out of our gravel drive, onto a paved road that wound down the mountainside, I took one last look at the house I'd called home. I was leaving everything I cared about behind. My brother's sleeping face flashed through my brain and fear lanced through my heart. He wouldn't understand why I left. But it was the only way to protect him. So long as I was there, Dean was in danger. But if I left, my father wouldn't have any leverage on me anymore. He wouldn't be able to use Dean to manipulate me into doing what he wanted.

I wasn't worried about Dean being forced to follow the path that I was trying to escape. The males of the family had a different role to play. The men went off into the world and made something of themselves. They were supposed to make alliances, deals, and uphold the traditions of the families. The women were just pawns in their game. It was backwards and patriarchal, something I had never understood. Especially given the free-spirited nature of my mother. I'd wanted to go to art school and pursue a career as an artist. But that was out of the question in my family. What dreams had she given up to marry to my father? I'd never know. She'd died when I was too young to ask those questions.

Before I could leave, though, I had one stop to make. One person, more than anyone, who would understand me leaving, though he could never know why. I gripped the steering wheel harder. More than anything, I wanted to tell him the truth and reveal the secret I'd been keeping. But to do that would mean driving an unforgivable wedge between us.

Cade would never understand why I did what I did. He would never forgive me for betraying him. And there was once a time where that wouldn't have mattered to me. He was a Black, and I was a Wild. Sworn enemies in a long-standing feud that had gone back generations since the very founding of the original city. Some even said that if it weren't for the Wild's wealth, this city would be called Black, Colorado instead.

I gripped the steering wheel tighter.

It was supposed to have been so simple. Gain his trust. Find out some useful information I could take back to my father and prove my loyalty. And then never think about Cade Black again.

Falling in love hadn't been part of the plan.

But that's exactly what had happened.

I'd fallen in love with the enemy.

And in doing so, I'd not only betrayed my family, I'd betrayed him.

So many nights I'd lay awake, the guilt of my betrayal keeping me from sleeping. But every time I opened my mouth to tell him the truth, fear squeezed my heart like a vice grip.

I couldn't lose him. I couldn't lose the one good thing in my life.

My father's words cut through me. Whore. Liar. A disgrace to my family. Those were the words he'd used when I'd told him I wouldn't betray Cade. I'd tried to get him to see reason. This feud was pointless and stupid. Our families had disagreed so long, no one even knew what they were fighting over. Just like that, a line in the mountain dirt had been drawn and on one side were the Blacks and on the other were the Wilds. There was no in-between.

"Choose," he'd said. "Your lover or your brother."

I'd looked at Dean and knew there was no other choice I could make. No other choice he would allow me to make.

My car was already packed. I'd been preparing for this moment for a very long time and had squirreled away little things here and there. Bess, our housekeeper and nanny, had helped me when and where she could. I'd hugged her one last time, my forehead bent to hers and whispered, "Take care of him, Bess. He won't understand. But neither of us will ever be free if I stay."

She'd squeezed me tight and kissed my cheek. "Go. Your mother would be so proud of you. I'll take care of the boy. I promise."

I mentally prepared myself for what I'd say to Cade. Would he come with me? Would he leave his father and everything they were trying to build for their family and escape? Could we just leave the history of our families, this place, this city, in the dust and start anew? I hoped so.

It was the only hope that I could cling to. That maybe one day we could move beyond "he's a Black and I'm a Wild, and therefore we shouldn't be together". Maybe one day I could even tell him the truth.

I watched as the old Fuller barn we would sneak away to meet in grew larger in the distance. Cade would be there waiting for me. I'd already sent him a text letting him know we needed to talk, and he hadn't answered me back, but I knew he'd be there. Cade was always there when I needed him.

The boy I'd been told was my worst enemy, had become the most stable and consistent person in my life. I'd been able to tell him my dreams, show him my artwork, and bask in his praise. Cade would share little bits of his life with his dad. His worry over his life as a member of a notorious motorcycle gang. The fear he had that he'd lose his dad to drugs and alcohol. He'd talk about the motorcycle shop he dreamed about opening with his dad someday, and the hope that once they finally got it off the ground, his dad would get clean and away from that life.

We'd spend every minute we could away from our families and with each other, riding down the mountain highways on the back of his bike. Escaping into the wildflower fields our city was known for, and for a moment in time, we were free.

That's what drew us together. We both wanted a different life than the one that had been planned out for us, simply because of what our last names were. And for the first time, someone had looked at me and hadn't seen "Juniper Wild, daughter of Edmund Wild, descendant of the original founders of this city and heir to the Wild legacy". To Cade, I was just Juniper. And to me, he was just Cade.

I pulled into the overgrown patch of dirt that the barn was sitting on and looked for Cade's red, classic Indian motorcycle, but I didn't see it there. Glancing down at my phone, I checked to see if he'd responded to my text, but only saw that he'd left it on read. I frowned. That wasn't like him.

Nerves made my palms sweat, and I opened the car door and got out, approaching the run-down barn. I didn't fear my dad finding out that I'd left. He was locked in his study for the night, working on a recent case. When he was engrossed in his work like that, I was basically ignored. No, my nerves had nothing to do with my father, and everything to do with the man I was meeting tonight.

He would come if he wasn't already here. Cade would come, and I would tell him the truth. I would confess everything, ask for his forgiveness, and beg him to leave with me. We could even take his dad and start over together.

No feud. No warring families. No judgement from the city or my father.

We'd be free.

2

JUNIPER

"Cade?"

The barn was quiet and dark, with the faint smell of old hay lingering in the air. It had sat unused for years until we'd made it our meeting place. So many days we'd met here, when I couldn't take another lecture, or another dinner where we'd all sat around the table in awkward silence. At least it had been awkward for me. Dean never seemed to notice the tension between us and he'd talk about his day, or something that happened at school, from the time we sat down until the last dish was cleared. Then our housekeeper would hustle him off to bed. Most of the time, my dad would ignore me and he'd go off to his study to finish up work. Sometimes he'd get a phone call from a client and he'd either not join us, or leave in the middle of dinner. Then it would be just me and Dean. Those nights were the best.

But on the other nights, the nights when he seemed the most intense, the most hawk-like, he'd pierce me with his gaze and begin grilling me on my life and my responsibilities as a Wild. Every word, every criticism, every insinuated disappointment, heaped onto my shoulders until it was all I could bear. I would never be the daughter he expected me to be.

"Cade?" my voice called out again in the darkness as I took a step further inside. I frowned. Was he here?

"Did you do this?"

A deep voice sounded from behind me and I jumped, startled by the gruffness of it, only to see Cade standing half in shadow, his face in a deep frown and his hazel eyes locked on me. My heart stuttered, just like it always did when I saw him. The moonlight filtered through a few broken slats of barn wood, highlighting a square jaw, full lips that begged to be kissed, and the hint of dimples when he smiled.

His voice came in low again, the frosty edge to it sending chills through me. I blinked, suddenly realizing that he wasn't smiling, as he held a paper up to the light filtering through the barn doors. "Do what?" I looked at the paper and took a step forward, but he shook his head, making me pause.

"Don't play with me, Juniper. You were the only one that knew about my dad's business deal." His hard gaze pierced me with the accusation, and I felt my heart sink. This couldn't be happening.

He shoved the paper in my face. "My dad's funding was denied without warning. No one else knew about it but me, the loan officer, and you. Tell me you didn't rat him out, Juniper."

I looked at the letter, hastily reading the few sentences, each one breaking my heart little by little. It was a letter from a small bank that stated they had denied his loan application due to 'moral turpitude'. Someone had forwarded them his rap sheet. My hands trembled as I read the words as tears threatened to fall.

"Cade, you don't understand. It's not what you think."

He cut me off. "Don't lie to me Juniper. I know it was you. Your father is the only one with the connections to pull a stunt like this." The venom in his voice slapped me and I gaped at him, shocked.

"Cade, I'm sorry. I didn't—" A sob caught in my throat as Cade turned his back to me, not listening to my pleas. My mind was reeling. This couldn't be happening. Not like this. My dad's voice whispered through my mind. "Choose."

"I heard your dad, Juniper, he came by the hardware store while I was at work and started talking to the Sheriff while he was there." He turned back around and took a step forward from the darkness, but it was as if the shadows clung to him. I shivered. I'd never seen this side of him. The part of him that had grown up as the son of a man deeply entrenched in a dangerous motorcycle gang, who had done hard things to survive. But I could see it now, the hostility, the inner rage just brimming beneath the surface. "He told the Sheriff how you'd finally come to your senses and how you'd proven your loyalty to the family."

I flinched, dread filling me. "Cade, please, let me explain. You can't believe him."

"How could I not? You're a Wild. Everything you do or have done is handed to you on a silver fucking platter. While I have to crawl in the dust for the scraps. You're a Wild and I'm a Black. Do you really think I don't know what's happening? That I don't see this for what it is? A good fucking time for little Miss Sunshine."

Pain lanced through my chest, and I struggled to

comprehend what he was saying. Each word drove a knife into my heart, deeper and harder than the last. We'd never talked much about the differences in our families. It would have destroyed the careful bubble we'd created so that we could be together in peace, without the history of our family feud coming into play. A bubble that crashed down around me as reality was creeping back in. "So you think just because my dad said it, it's true?"

Cade snorted. "I'd sooner believe a snake in the grass than anything out of Edmund Wild's mouth. But then, when my dad came home saying they had denied him the loan, I knew the truth. Only one person has the influence in this city to force them to not give him the money. And that is Mr. Edmund D. Wild. Your dad."

He took another step forward. "When were you going to tell me about the engagement?"

"Wh-what?" I stuttered, my lips trembling as I tried to hold back a sob and involuntarily backed away from him.

"I heard a lot more than just bragging about how proud he was of you. You've been running around getting your rocks off, being the rebellious princess with me, but playing the 'good girl' at home." My back hit a barn pole as he closed in on me and his arms came up to either side of it, caging me in. "Tell me something, pretty girl. Were you going to wait to fuck me before or after the wedding?"

I gasped at the dark timbre of his voice and the closeness of our bodies, as the heat he radiated sank into my skin. Even with him raging. Even with the weapon of his words, cutting me over and over again. I wanted him. His eyes darkened as if he sensed the shift in me and he leaned down, burying his nose into my neck, inhaling my scent. His lips barely brushed against my jaw as he growled into my ear.

"You've been throwing yourself at me for the past year, practically begging me to fuck you. And I've held back because you were Juniper. My Juniper. And you were too good, too perfect. I wanted to wait, not because I didn't want you." He rolled his hips against me and I felt the bulging hardness beneath his jeans. Heat coursed through me and I tipped my head back, instinctively reaching for him, but he held still, keeping his lips a hair's breadth away from my skin. "Because I didn't want to spoil you with my brokenness. But I guess we don't need to worry about that now, do we?"

"I'm not good, or perfect, Cade. And I never

asked you to be. I just wanted you. Only you." My heart stuttered with the dark pain his words echoed.

He chuckled darkly. "You're a pretty little liar, Juniper Wild. But that's ok. Because I'm going to do what I should have done all along. Your father taught me a valuable lesson today." He brought one of his hands down to trace the edge of my jean skirt, leaving a trail of heat where his fingers brushed against my skin. His hand slid upward, stopping to pull at the lace edge of my panties.

"What lesson?" I whispered, trying to hold my body still even though all I wanted to do was scream at him to continue. The few times we'd fooled around, Cade had always held back when I'd wanted more, and in my foolish, girlish mind, I'd thought he just hadn't been ready. I'd never considered that he hadn't thought himself good enough for me.

He pulled back and looked down at me, his eyes burning pools of green, jade, and liquid gold. A dark ring lined his pupils, framed by long, dark lashes. He was a work of art.

"That when you want something, you take it." And then his fingers plunged into me, filling and stretching in a way that I'd never felt before. My head fell back against the rough wood of the barn pole and I moaned.

His eyes widened in surprise for a brief second as he felt the slick heat and wetness around his fingers, as if he was shocked by the obvious sign of my desire for him. And then, as if a switch had been flipped, he growled and pressed into me again, his fingers plunging over and over into my welcoming heat.

My arms came up to wrap around his neck as I pulled him in closer. I wanted, needed, more of him. "Cade..." I moaned his name like a prayer, and then my voice was swallowed as he answered it with a punishing, bruising kiss.

"I'm not stopping this time, Juniper Wild. You're going to get what you want and so am I. You might never have been mine, but I'll make damn sure you'll never want to be anyone else's." His words were a sinister promise against my lips as his fingers continued to tease my opening. He alternated between filling me with his fingers and circling the tender nub of flesh until I was a soaking mess against his hand.

I sobbed as his fingers filled me again and his palm ground against my clit. "I don't want anyone else, Cade. I never did."

"Don't. Fucking. Lie." He snarled, and suddenly I was being lifted and carried to a darker corner of the barn. My back hit the ground as he set me down, but a stash of blankets we'd hidden there minimized the impact. I heard the rustle of clothes, the slide of a belt through jeans, and then hands sliding up my bare thighs once more, pushing my skirt higher and higher. My breath caught when I felt the smooth skin of his jaw brush against my inner thigh as he pulled aside my panties, exposing me. Then his mouth and tongue replaced where his fingers had been moments before, filling me, lapping at me, driving me to the brink of insanity.

I arched against him and cried out. "Cade!" It was too much. Too much pleasure, too much feeling, too much of everything. But he didn't stop. All he did was growl and spread my thighs further apart, then plunged his fingers back into my pussy as his lips and teeth attacked my clit.

Nothing prepared me for the explosion that would rack through my body. I heard Cade's name being screamed in the distance and belatedly; I realized I was the one doing it.

"That's it, pretty girl. Scream my name. And every time he touches, fucks, or so much as looks at you…remember this."Then he was over me, his thick hardness pressing against my opening, but he paused and my eyes flew open to see him staring down at where his cock was lined up with my pussy. He looked back at me, a hesitation in his eyes, and pain. So much pain and anger. This was Cade laid bare.

"This will hurt." I could see it then. He was giving me an out. A moment to reject him fully, to make true everything my father ever said about him, about us. I arched my hips to his, not giving him time to pull away, and then he was filling me, stretching me, tearing through me as his cock plunged into my heat. It burned, and I gasped. He stilled for a moment, giving me time to adjust, but I didn't want him to stop. I wanted all of it, the pain, the hurt, the punishment. I wanted him. So I wrapped my legs around his waist, pulled him in closer, and sealed my mouth to his.

Something took over, and he moved, driving his hips downward into mine. Drawing out and plunging back in. Filling me over and over again in a driving, punishing rhythm. The pressure built again, slower, deeper this time, and I moaned, my hands twisting in his hair as I tried to chase the feeling with him.

Suddenly his mouth left mine, as my shirt and bra were jerked up, exposing my breasts. He groaned against my flesh, his tongue circling one sensitive bud and drawing it into his mouth. I cried out as he bit down with his teeth, the pain and pleasure combining in a way I'd never experienced before. With his other hand, he pinched and rolled my other nipple, the two sensations nearly overwhelming me.

It was almost too much again. "Cade, please..." I wasn't sure what I was begging for, only that I needed it from him.

He rose, grabbing my hands that were pulling at his hips, demanding him to give me what I wanted, and pinned them above my head.

"You don't get to tell me what to do, pretty girl. I told you I was taking what I wanted." He growled and slammed his cock into me, filling me deeper than before. Wetness pooled between us and I panted.

"You can't take what was always yours to begin with."

He stilled and then, just as suddenly as he'd begun, he was withdrawing from me and I felt the cold emptiness of his absence.

"You could never be mine." His voice was like ice. "Go home, Juniper."

I lay there, clothes skewed, the wetness and something more sticking to my thighs, and watched as he stood, drawing his pants back up.

A creeping numbness settled over my skin. I'd done this. I'd betrayed him. My father's words whispered once more, like a sinister omen through my mind. "Choose."

Only there was no choice. There never would be for me because my father held all the control. And he'd just shown how far that control reached.

My Cade.

My safety and refuge.

But not anymore.

My heart shattered, and my body reacted before my mind knew what it was doing. I scrambled to my feet, tugging my clothes back into place and I ran. I ran right back to my sunshine yellow VW, Cade's voice calling out to me, but I couldn't hear or understand him beyond the sobs and rush of blood in my ears. I started the car, jerked it into gear, and hit the gas pedal, the gears grinding and gravel flying as I sped away.

I didn't look back.

3

CADE

The minute the words left my mouth I regretted them. They tasted like bile on my tongue, but that's exactly how I'd felt for the past several hours as I'd sat with my dad and tried to talk him off another bender. As Juniper ran, I tried to get her to stop, to apologize, but she wasn't listening and all I could hear was the slurred speech of my dad's voice in my ear as he faded in and out of consciousness.

"Lost it, buddy. Lost it all."

Rage took me again and I whirled to slam my fist into the nearest thing, which just happened to be the side of the barn. Pain reverberated up my arm and I knew I'd done some damage, but at this point, I didn't care. Everything was falling apart. Everything.

I hadn't wanted to believe that Juniper would let slip that my dad was starting up his own motorcycle shop, but then I'd seen the way Mr. Wild had looked at me as he was speaking, a knowing smirk twisting at his lips. I knew then that he'd found out, and there was only one person he could have learned it from, his daughter. One slip of the tongue was all it took for him to pounce. I'd stormed out of the shop, not even bothering to finish with my orders for the day. Every fiber in my being wanted to stand up and pound his face to a pulp for the way he talked about my dad, and the way he treated Juniper. Like she was some sort of property he could barter with. I hadn't even told her half of what I'd overheard him say. No. What he *wanted* me to hear.

That Juniper was already bought and paid for in some backward family deal. That he'd basically used her as a bargaining chip with one of his clients so that he could elevate his own status. And that Juniper would acquiesce because she wouldn't have a choice. She might run off with me for a short time, but give her a month and she'd be crawling back, begging for her father's forgiveness. She was a Wild and I was a Black. We were destined to be on the opposite ends of the social circle since the day our families had shown up and staked claim to this patch of mountain dirt. I didn't know much about the reasons or why it had come to be this way. Just that it always was. And so long as my last name was Black, her father would never approve of us being together.

All those thoughts. All the words Edmund Wild had said. The way his lips curled in a sneer. My father passed out, a fifth of cheap whiskey half-spilled down the secondhand suit he'd worn, for the bank interview he didn't even get to go to. Juniper's wide, innocent expression as she told me she'd never betrayed me. It was like a slap in the face as I realized that she was lying to my face. All of it had spewed out of me.

This was her fault. And my fault for thinking it could ever work between us. For loving her.

"Lost it. Lost it all, buddy." My dad's words echoed again and again.

I stormed across an overgrown path to where I'd parked my bike, cranking it up with a roar of the engine and the squeal of tires and gravel. And then I was flying. The sound of the road and the wind in my ears drowned out his words. Part of me wanted to follow after Juniper. Get her to admit she'd made a mistake. Apologize for losing my temper. For taking her the way I did. Guilt twisted in my gut.

Gravel road gave way to blacktop and I flew down the mountain interstate. I didn't pay attention to mile markers or time. The scenery bled past me in a kaleidoscope of colors. Colors Juniper would have wanted to stop and wonder at in amazement, or force me over to the side of the freeway to whip out her pencils and sketch. But I didn't see them. All I could see was black asphalt, the white lines blurring, and the red and blue lights flashing in my side mirrors. Wait. Red and blue lights. I glared and checked my speedometer. 120mph. Fuck. I slowed down and pulled over.

The highway patrol car came to a stop behind me and I crossed my arms, waiting. A dark shadow blocked the sun. "Well if it isn't David Black's boy." The gravely voice that sounded like he was one cigar away from lung cancer grated on my ears.

"Sheriff Joley. Surprised to see you out here on road duty." I tried to give him a charming smile. The Sheriff wasn't actually a bad man, even if he was in Edmund Wild's pocket. He'd given me a warning and let me off the hook more times than I could count, I was hoping that this would be another of those times.

The Sheriff didn't smile back, just stared at me beneath his bushy gray eyebrows. There was a tension about him I had never seen before, and as I finally took in his whole stance, I realized he'd kept one hand on the gun at his side. My smile waned. "Look, Sheriff, I know what you're going to say and I'm sorry, I wasn't paying attention."

"Were you coming from the Foster barn?" His question threw me for a loop and I frowned in confusion.

"Well, yeah...I mean that general direction." The Foster barn was on the same property as the run-down barn Juniper and I met at, just a little further down the road and closer to their ranch.

"When was the last time you spoke to Jim Foster?" Even more confused, I glanced back at the patrol car, to see one of the sheriff's deputies speaking into his radio before he opened the door and stepped out. Jim Foster was the bank manager and son of Dave Foster, the man who owned the ranch.

"I don't even know Jim. Sheriff, can you tell me what this is about? Is it the speeding? Because I'll pay the ticket."

"Hold out your hands, son." The sheriff ordered,

his gruff voice no-nonsense and the hair on the back of my neck rose.

"Sheriff Joley, I don't know what you're getting at here but there's got to be some kind of a misunderstanding. I was just speeding." I heard the deputy behind me step closer.

"You heard the sheriff. Hold out your hands."

I held out my hands and the sheriff glanced down, his bushy brows coming together in a deep frown as he took in my bruised and cut-up right hand. "Son, I'm afraid I'm going to have to ask you to come with me."

By now the sun was setting, but I felt more than the chill of the Colorado air seep under the leather of my jacket.

"Are you arresting me?"

The Sheriff gave me a stony expression. "That depends. Can anyone vouch for your whereabouts in the last hour?"

I felt a small wave of relief. Juniper. But would she help me after what I'd done? "Yeah, Juniper was with me. She can verify where I was."

"Hmmm..." Was the only sound the Sheriff made and he gave a nod to the deputy who got back on his radio. The minutes ticked by, agonizingly slow, and then the deputy muttered his thanks and shook his head. "No one can get a hold of Miss Wild."

The relief I'd felt, disappeared just as quickly as it came. Where was Juniper? Was she ok? Fear and guilt spiraled through my thoughts. I needed to find Juniper and make sure she was ok. What the fuck had I been thinking taking her like that? Making her first time on the barn floor? The Sheriff just nodded and turned back to me. For a moment I thought I saw him hesitate, but then he stiffened and reached for his cuffs. "Cade Black, you're under arrest for arson and attempted murder. Please put your hands behind your back."

The words hit me like a ton of bricks and it felt like the world around me began to spiral. I swayed on my feet as the deputy grabbed me and hauled me against the patrol car. As I felt the impact of the cold metal and my arms were wrenched behind my back, I began to struggle and turned to the Sheriff.

"Sheriff, I don't know what you think I did, but I swear I didn't. Find Juniper. She was with me. She can vouch for me." *And I need to make this right. I need to fix it.* The deputy kicked my legs apart and slammed me harder against the patrol car. It took everything I had to resist the urge to fight his overly-aggressive tactics. He was definitely going a little harder than needed for the sake of his boss.

The Sheriff stared at me for a moment, then shook his head, with a resigned sigh he said, "I hope for your sake, you're right, Cade. Because she's the only one that can save you right now. The only one..."

4

JUNIPER

ive years later...

"Come on bro, you can do this." The whispered words hit my ears and I blinked, unsure if I had just imagined it, or in my slightly-inebriated state, had misheard the statement. I gave a little moan and then rolled my hips sensually. Maybe the guy just needed a little encouragement. I felt the whisper of hands on my thighs, and then a deep breath was inhaled as he buried his nose against my skin. The skin of my knee to be precise. He groaned, only it wasn't the kind of groan a woman expects to hear from a man who promised to give her the ride of her life, with just his tongue. "Just do it bro. It's just like mushrooms."

I sat up and looked down, immediately regretting that decision. The guy looked like he was going to be sick. His eyes were shut, tight and he was gripping the sheet bunched between my legs like it was a lifeline.

"Did you just compare me to mushrooms?"

There was no way I'd had enough drinks to have misheard that statement. In fact, the longer this went on, the more sober I was becoming. He popped up, his eyes wide with shock and embarrassment.

"Oh shit, no— no that's not what I mean. You aren't like mushrooms at all. I just don't like mushrooms. Or, I didn't. Until my therapist told me to eat them and now I *love* mushrooms."

I tried to rewind the events of the past few weeks, in order to understand just how I'd gotten into this position. Half-undressed in my tiny studio apartment, with the guy who'd been hitting on me for ages at my bar, kneeling between my open thighs with the most horrified expression on his face. *Stacy.* That's right. Miss busy-body, thinks-she-knows-it-all best friend, Stacy, had done this. She'd been yapping at me since I'd dumped my last boyfriend, saying that I needed to get out and start dating people again, and somehow I'd decided to give-in with the sweet, persistent, if not somewhat bland, guy. Sweet, persistent, just-compared-me-to-mushrooms, guy. Wait, did he say his *therapist?*

"Hold on, what does your therapist and mushrooms have to do with all…" I reached down to pull the sheet up over my overly-embarrassed and very-underwhelmed, lady parts. "…this."

His eyes rounded in what I once would have described as a cute and innocent puppy-dog expression, but he'd just compared eating me out, to eating mushrooms, and I wasn't exactly feeling all that benevolent anymore.

"Ok so, you know how I go to weekly therapy sessions." I nodded, it had actually been one of the things about him, Brian, that had made me feel safe with testing the waters in the dating scene again. My last few picks had been rodeos of selfish, narcissistic, ass-holes. It seemed I liked the bad-boy type but not the bad-boy drama that came with it. So when he'd walked into my bar with his clean-cut look and big, brown eyes, I'd finally given in to Stacy's nagging and accepted his offer for a date. One nice date had led to several more, and then here we were, finally getting beyond the goodnight kiss at the door, and he'd somehow brought mushrooms and therapy into it. Talk about a mood-killer.

"Well," he continued on, oblivious to my souring mood. "My therapist said that I needed to start approaching things that I hate with a new attitude. Start testing it out and see if maybe I don't like it because I genuinely don't like it, or because I've just never tried it before. Like mushrooms."

I arched a brow and tried to keep my voice from showing any of my annoyance. "Ok, so you're saying you don't like giving oral, or you just have never done it before to know if you like it or not?" I was trying not to judge too quickly here. Maybe he was just inexperienced and genuinely didn't know. Maybe I'd be thanking his therapist later for pointing him in the right direction.

He laughed, "Oh no, I hate it. I mean, I like getting it." He winked. "But I've just never really thought of it as a necessary part of sex, ya know? It's just not my thing."

I stared at him while my brain tried to process what he just said.

"And just what else isn't 'your thing'?" I honestly wasn't sure I wanted to know the answer, but the words were out of my mouth before I could take them back, and I was going to blame *that* on the tequila, and Stacy as well. He didn't seem to notice the acid dripping from my voice.

"Oh well, to be honest, going to the bar where you work wasn't really my thing either. But look how it turned out." He grinned at me and leaned in to place a kiss on my shoulder, but I pulled away.

"Wait, are you saying even coming to my bar was part of your therapy?" The way he glanced away and then back at me set off alarm bells. "Hold on, are you *really* getting this advice from an *actual* therapist?"

He turned those puppy-dog brown eyes back towards me and I suddenly thought they looked less like a puppy, and more like a guy who was feeding me a bunch of bullshit.

"Ok well, it's more of this guy I follow on TikTok. I bought a course from him." He rushed on. "But he's a relationship coach and seriously has helped lots of guys like me get the life they've always wanted."

I blinked, stunned. "You're getting therapy and relationship advice from a guy on social media?"

"Well, yeah, who has time for actual therapy? Plus this guy knows what I'm going through. How hard it is to be a man now, and what it means to be an alpha-male. It seriously has changed my life. I'd have never been able to pull a hot chick like you, without his advice." He licked his lips and reached for me again, but I was scrambling to stand up while pulling the sheet with me.

"Ok, Brian, I appreciate your attempts to uh— *better yourself*. But I think in the future, you might want to speak to an *actual* therapist, and maybe not ever—and I mean this with all sincerity, refer to oral sex with a woman as *eating mushrooms*."

Brian stood with me and frowned as I marched over to my door, placing my hand on the knob. He was still half-undressed and it took every bit of politeness I had left in me, not to ask him to just leave in his boxer-briefs. Fortunately for him, he didn't say anything as he gathered up his clothes and items. When he got to the door he paused as if he wanted to make a statement, but instead just shook his head and left. As I closed the door, I was sure I could hear him muttering something about females not understanding the complexity of men's brains, but I just didn't have the energy left to deal with it. I was sure he was already on TikTok making some sad video about how a man can't be vulnerable with a woman because we would just judge their insecurities.

"Fucking mushrooms." If I hadn't been so pissed at myself, and Stacy, I might have laughed at the absurdity of it. I knew I shouldn't have gone out with the guy. But just like he was trying to get out of his comfort zone and try something new, so was I. The only difference is that I didn't need a TikTok therapist, or anyone else, to tell me what I was running from.

Not what, but who.

It had been five years since I'd last seen or heard from Cade Black, yet his presence still hung like a shadow around every guy I'd dated, or even thought about dating. There had been a few that had almost made me forget, until inevitably they'd say or do something that had me comparing them to Cade, and then it was goodbye new relationship and hello *Netflix and Chill* nights for one.

My phone buzzed on my tiny coffee table and I lunged for it, nearly tripping over the sheets I still had wrapped around my waist. It was Stacy. Good, just the person I wanted to rant to, and also threaten with her life if she ever encouraged me to jump back into the dating pool again.

I hit the button and started to speak, "You will *not* believe what just happened."

"Oh shit. I can tell just by your tone it didn't go well, and I *promise* I want to hear all about it, but you're going to have to tell me on your way down to the bar." Her voice sounded rushed, and I could hear a commotion in the background above the normal, loud, thumping music that was playing.

I tucked the phone between my shoulder and cheek, dropping the sheet from around my waist as I began to hunt for my pants. "What do you mean? What's the issue?"

"Umm, well, remember how you told Jax that if he ever came back here you'd encase his balls in glass and wear them like earrings?"

I groaned. Tonight was not the night that I wanted to deal with another reminder of failed relationships. "Yes. You mean he's there? Can't you just give him a shot of whiskey and let him go on his way?"

"No. He's insisting that he only gets served by you and uh, he's got some friends with him. Some really really not-nice looking friends." Something in Stacy's tone made me pause. She sounded scared.

I finished pulling my pants up, grabbing my shoes and wallet. "I'll be right there."

I heard an audible sigh of relief. "Ok," she said. "I'll try and distract them until you get here."

Opening my apartment door I headed out into the hall. "Ok and Stacy, whatever you do, do *not* call the boss. Jax is my problem. I'll handle it."

## 5

### JUNIPER

*Club Diablo* was a five-story behemoth. Each layer of the club was a different theme, with the lowest floor reserved for the roughest of crowds. The motorcycle gangs that worked the dark streets of Denver's crime scenes. I pulled across the street to the employee parking and sighed, taking in the dark monstrosity. If someone had told me five years ago that I'd be the head bartender at a biker bar owned by one of the most notorious businessmen in Denver, while freelancing as a tattoo artist on the side for cash, I'd have laughed in their face and accused them of being on one hell of an acid trip. But here I was, five years after leaving the small city I grew up in, doing just that.

Not painting, not traveling and seeing my art

hung in galleries around the world. It felt like those dreams were a whole other life now. Like that was a different Juniper than the one who was standing outside a dirty biker bar right now.

I slammed the car door shut and looked down at my girl. She was a little worse for the wear five years later, but she still ran.

After I'd left Cade, I'd just drove, not stopping until I'd hit the first city that was big enough where I could just disappear to. I'd had thoughts of going out of state, somewhere far away, but I'd left with nothing but the clothes on my back, and the little bit of money I'd managed to save. Denver was big enough that I knew my dad would have a hard time finding me. The plan had been to get a job, get money, and get out. Only, it was much harder than I'd thought to find work under the table, that paid enough to pay the bills and keep you fed. I'd managed to scrape together enough of a life here that I could survive. But the plans to leave for good always seemed to get pushed to the back burner.

No one here knew me as Juniper Wild, heiress to the Wild legacy, daughter of Edmund Wild. I wasn't an aspiring painter and artist with dreams of seeing the world, and capturing all the colors and beauty I found there. Here, in the seedy underground of

Denver's biker bars and motorcycle clubs, I was just June. Bartender extraordinaire and terrible picker-of-men.

I sighed and made my way across the street to the back entrance meant just for employees. There was a bouncer stationed outside the door, just in case an unruly customer decided to try their luck sneaking back inside once they'd been kicked out. I nodded to Big Jim, where he leaned against the brick wall, and received a grunt in return.

"Thought you had the night off for a date or sumthin'..." He growled around a wad of tobacco that sat like a permanent golf ball in his lip. Big Jim really wasn't all that big. I'd once made the mistake of asking him where he got his nickname from, and all he'd done was spit into his dip bottle and leer at me with an "I'll give you one guess lil' darlin'." Fortunately, it was the only time he'd made any kind of pass at me, and instead preferred to spend his time complaining about the hours he worked, or the 'ol' lady' who was bitching at him at home.

"I did. Didn't work out." I really didn't want to get into the details of my failed date, and was hoping this was going to be one of those nights where Big Jim wasn't in the mood to chat, and he'd just let me in so I could slip inside and deal with the Jax situation.

Jim shook his head, launching a wad of spit to the side before narrowing his beady eyes at me. "I could have told you that. That guy was a boot-licking pea-brain, not the kind of man you need."

I cocked my head and tried to give him a polite smile, hoping that if I appeased him, he'd decide he was tired of talking and let me in. "Well, thank you for that assessment Jim. I think we can both agree on that."

Jim nodded as if somehow he'd managed to impart some great life lesson to me. "Yep. You ain't the kind of girl that needs to be shacking up with one of them lowlifes in the Pit, either. In-fact—" He straightened, as if somehow my agreeing with him had given him some sort of authority, then gave me a once-over from head to toe while nodding to himself like he'd just confirmed his own thoughts. "You shouldn't even be working in there, June-girl. Yer just askin' to be brought down to their level. Why don't you talk to Mr. Diovolo about moving up to one of them fancy restaurants he has across the city? I'll even call him for you. He don't know what he's doing putting you in this place." He shook his head and began to reach for his cellphone as if he was going to call the man right that very second. "Just a waste."

"No!" I reached out and quickly put my hand on his wrist to stop him from hitting the *send* button. Jim looked at me in surprise, and I tried to calm my racing heart. The last person I needed or wanted attention from, was Kage Diovolo. Mr. Diovolo was not just a prominent businessman in Denver, but he was also the rumored head of a notorious biker gang. I wasn't sure what connections Mr. Diovolo had, but I knew that there was a good chance he ran in the same circles that my father did. And a man who had risen to the top like he had, didn't get there by being an idiot. A few well-placed inquiries, and he'd figure out who my father was, then my newfound freedom would be over and I'd be on the run again. The only reason I'd decided to take the risk was because I was sure a place like Club Diablo was the last place my father would have come looking.

When I'd first interviewed for the job here as a shot girl and waitress, Kage had nearly made me piss myself with his intensity. But I was desperate. I couldn't put my name down on any financial forms, working under the table was the only hope I had to make money. But when Kage had offered me a position as one of his escorts, I'd drawn the line. I didn't care how scary or powerful he was. I wasn't going to be bought and sold. I wouldn't do it as Juniper Wild and I wouldn't do it as plain old June.

Somehow, I'd managed to tell him that without giving away too much of my past. He'd been a stone-cold wall of silence as he'd listened to me plead my case and then, when I was done, all he said was, "If you cause me any trouble, and I mean *any* trouble, I'll find out who you really are and no one will ever hear from you again. Do you understand?"

The rest was history. I'd worked my way up from shot girl to bartender, to eventually becoming the head bartender. Things had been going great and I'd kept my promise to never cause trouble. Until now.

"Big Jim, I like my job. I like working here and you're right, all the guys here are losers." I grinned and winked at him. "Except you, of course. But you're taken and I don't need Linda coming after me, accusing me of trying to steal her man." When logic and reason didn't work, flirting and flattery almost always did. I watched as Big Jim's ears turned red, and he huffed, spitting another pile of green goo into his dip cup.

"Well, I'm too old for you anyway. But seriously, you think about what I said. Mr. Diovolo will help get you out of here and in the right places. He's got connections." Jim moved to the side and hit the code to unlock the door, as I sighed inwardly with relief.

I ducked into the dark corridor and cast an appreciative smile over my shoulder. "Thanks Jim, but I'm fine right where I am, for now. Wild horses couldn't drag me away."

The door was slammed shut behind me, and I was left in the back stockroom of the lowest level of Club Diablo, a bar that had been affectionately and most accurately named "The Pit".

A purple-haired, brown-eyed ball of energy wearing a *Def Leppard* ripped t-shirt, short, denim shorts over neon yellow fishnet stockings and black, platform boots that added a good four inches to her five-foot frame, bounced into the room and gave me a wide-eyed look.

"Oh thank God you're here. Jax was threatening to go get you himself if you didn't show up soon." Stacy's hands twisted the giant stone plugs that hung from her ears, a nervous habit she had, and probably one of the reasons she had so many piercings to begin with. She was pierced in places I hadn't thought possible. I always teased her about being a metal detector's worst nightmare, but I couldn't imagine her without them. They were what made Stacy, Stacy.

I snorted and hung my leather jacket up, then pulled my blonde hair into a high ponytail before grabbing my makeup bag for a quick touch up. "I seriously doubt he'd want to try that again, since I ran him off with my gun shoved in his nutsack."

A glance in the tiny mirror outside of my work locker told me I still had 'date' makeup on. It was a far cry from the normal biker chick look I went for when I was working, but it would have to do. I didn't go as far as Stacy did with my style, preferring to stick to black tank tops and ripped jeans or shorts, but I'd learned a little extra war paint made for a great disguise for when I was off the clock and I didn't want customers recognizing me.

Giving myself one last glance over, I turned to where the loud, thumping, rock music was coming from, as Jim's reprimand about not dating anymore of the lowlifes who frequented The Pit, came back to me. I hated to admit it, but the old biker was right. No more mixing work and business, no matter how badly I wanted to get laid.

6

JUNIPER

I pushed open the swinging door that led to the bar and was immediately assaulted with the screaming sounds of heavy metal guitars, a growling singer and the loud din of male voices trying to shout their orders at the overwhelmed bartenders, who were hustling and slinging drinks like they were some sort of bartending ninjas.

The Pit was normally loud and rowdy on a weekend night, but it was a Wednesday and this was unusually busy. I tried to think of any biker events or concerts that might warrant the sudden influx of customers, but I knew there was nothing on the calendar. As the head bartender it was my job to make sure the waitstaff was scheduled and prepared so they didn't get overwhelmed. But what I was witnessing tonight was almost pure pandemonium.

My eyes narrowed as I saw a tall, blonde-haired man leaning against the main bar with the seats on either side of him completely vacant.

Jax.

The bar was so crowded, I knew those seats weren't just abandoned or waiting for their occupants to return. The asshole was being purposely rude and holding the bar stools hostage from other guests. I glanced at the unfamiliar men surrounding Jax, who were occupying the remaining barstools and frowned. They must have been Jax's new friends that Stacy mentioned, and she was right. They did not look very nice.

I was used to dealing with the tough biker crowd after working at The Pit for so long. But these guys took *rough around the edges* to a whole new level.

As if Jax could sense me watching him, his head snapped in my direction and he leaned back against the space where he was holding court, with a condescending grin spreading across his handsome face. I inwardly cringed as I remembered that at one time, I'd thought that smile had been panty-melting hot. Jax had been the first guy since Cade that had made me want to try a relationship again. Others had been flings and one-night stands. Once I'd gotten to Denver, I'd gone through a bit of what I liked to call a "self-discovery phase". Essentially, discovering all the things I liked and didn't like about myself. Including sex.

It had been one more way for me to separate myself from who I was as Juniper Wild. It had been one more way I could build a wall between the girl who'd been in love and the woman who was trying to forget.

Jax had hit me with all the sexy, dangerous charm a naïve small-city girl couldn't resist. Flattery and attention that had my head spinning, and me running to jump on the back of his bike anytime he snapped his bad-boy fingers. He'd opened my eyes to a life of underground parties, wild, midnight rides and the dark underbelly of the biker gang world.

It had been hot, intense, and full of danger. It had also been completely one-sided, and I learned the hard way that I wasn't the only girl he'd been showing the dark side of life to.

After one memorable night where I'd been caught between Jax and some guy he'd pissed off in a dice game, I decided that my dance with danger was over. I'd naively thought that Jax would agree with me and somehow just walk away from all of it. But it turned out all he did was walk right into the arms of the next girl. Or rather, her mouth.

Because that's how I'd discovered he'd always had an alternate or two waiting in the wings. I'd walked into the employee bathroom of The Pit to see him with his legs spread, hands behind his head, pants down around his ankles and some girl on her knees doing her best porn star performance. Gag effects and all.

I'd been so shocked that I'd just stared, unblinking, until Jax had opened his baby blue eyes, and with a condescending smirk, asked if I'd like to join them.

The same condescending smirk he had on his face now. I glared at him and grabbed a bottle opener as I made my way over. Apparently, Jax hadn't quite gotten the message about where his balls were going to end up if he came anywhere near me again.

"If you aren't using those seats, they need to be given to customers who are waiting, Jax." The music was loud, but I knew he'd heard me. He looked down and did a slow, sensual once over. It was the kind of look that would have had me hot and bothered at one time, but now all I felt was revulsion. I would have preferred mushroom guy to Jax at the moment.

"Come on June, baby. I was just saving a seat for you. I know you're not on shift tonight. Have a drink with me." He patted one of the empty stools.

I shook my head. "Jax, I wouldn't have a drink with you if the world was on fire and you held the last water bottle. Now, either give up the seats to *actual* customers and leave, or— actually, no, that's it. Just give up the seats and leave, please."

Jax folded his arms across his broad chest and looked at the men to the left and the right of him. "Oh, I don't think so, baby. I think we'll stay right here." He turned his gaze back to me and his smirk hardened. "And you're going to serve us a few rounds." He leaned down until his eyes were almost level with mine, as he enunciated his words. "On. The. House."

I let out a very unladylike snort, not letting his intimidation tactics get to me. "And why the hell would I do that, Jax? You still haven't paid me back from the last time you ran up a bar tab with your friends."

Jax leaned in closer, his lips coming to brush against my ear, and it took everything in me not to put space between us as he whispered huskily. "Because I know who you are. And I know who would pay me *a lot* of money to find out where his sweet girl is, *Juniper Wild.*' He leaned back and gave me a wink. The music and the noise from the bar faded into the background, as I stared into the eyes of the man who'd just dropped a bomb into my otherwise peaceful world.

Jax knew who I was.

Which meant someone he associated with also knew who I was.

This was not good.

Other than a few stolen conversations with friends back in Wild to check on my brother, I'd not had contact with anyone from the city since I'd left. I'd honestly thought my dad had given up on me, choosing to concentrate on his remaining heir instead. But it seemed years of silence had meant nothing other than I'd just been given a reprieve.

Something in my look must have made him realize just how much of the upper hand he had, because he gave me a sympathetic look and brushed a stray strand of hair from my face.

"Oh baby, don't give me that look. I won't let anything happen to you. I'm the only one that knows. And it's going to stay that way, so long as we can come to a little agreement." He smiled and patted the barstool next to him again. I gave a glance to the nasty-looking bikers on the left and right of him before inching closer to the stool, but chose not to sit.

"Who told you and who are these guys you're with, Jax? I don't recognize them." I twisted the bottle opener in my hand nervously, as all the scenarios flew through my head. Could I trust Jax to keep my secret? Possibly, so long as there was something in it for him. I watched as he waved down a harried bartender and ordered a shot of our top-shelf whiskey. I wasn't going to be able to afford to keep him fed on whiskey for long though, and knowing Jax, he wouldn't be content with just whiskey for much longer. I gripped the bottle opener tighter.

"Oh, you hear things you know. I know some *very* powerful people." He gave me another wink, draining the whiskey before slamming the glass back down and signaling for another. I grimaced.

"As for these guys, well, let's just say they have a vested interest in me and my well-being." He slammed the shot again and leaned in closer to me, his hot, whiskey breath fanning my face, and I tried not to gag. "Which means they will have a vested interest in you now, too."

One of the men must have heard a snippet of our conversation because he snorted. "Our interest in you is *temporary."* He was a burly man with a close-shaved head and a tiny skull engulfed in flames, tattooed next to his eye. Jax glared at him and looked as if he was about to argue, but then the man stood up and gave him a look that sent chills down my spine, before slamming a few twenties on the counter and walking away. I turned back to Jax and arched a brow.

"Wow, they seem very. What was the word you used? 'Vested'?" I sneered at him and watched as an embarrassed flush spread up his neck. Jax prided himself on his reputation and hated when someone mocked him or made him look bad. He leaned in and grabbed my arm, beginning to pull me away from the bar. "Come on, we're leaving. You have something I need," He growled and swayed on his feet. Apparently, the whiskey was hitting him hard.

I planted my feet and shrugged out of his grasp.

"I'm not going anywhere with you, Jax."

He glared at me, his blue eyes darkening with anger. "Yes. You. Are." He took a step towards me and I felt my back hit the bar as he crowded my space. "You are going to come with me and do *everything* I tell you to. I own you now Juniper Wild. You think your dad finding out where you are is the worst thing in life? I can promise you, there are much, much nastier things waiting for you if you don't do what I say."

A wave of fear, followed by a dark and glittering rage flooded through me, before I knew what had happened, I'd closed the gap between us. His eyes widened in shock as I leaned up on my tiptoes and growled in his face. "No one owns me, Jaxon. Not my dad. Not you. Not anyone." I looked down to where I'd taken the bottle opener and shoved it into his crotch so hard, that the tip had pierced his jeans and was now jammed right into his balls. He stumbled back in pain, but I grabbed his jacket, pulled him closer and shoved the bottle opener harder into the tender flesh. I wasn't letting Jax take me anywhere.

He dropped to the floor the minute I let go of his jacket and I quickly stepped over him, leaving the bottle opener firmly planted in his crotch, then quickly made my way through the crowd looking for an escape.

I tried not to look behind me as I heard the commotion from Jax's screaming start to gain traction. Stacy's purple hair bobbed in my peripheral vision, and I turned to see her waving at me frantically. She was holding an emergency exit open, and I sighed with relief. Leave it to Stacy to be able to read a room and know when to bail. I rushed towards her.

"Thank God. I have to get out of here."

Stacy gave me a worried look. "I don't know what's going on, but you've got more than just Jax to deal with. I'll stall as long as possible, but there's someone in the alley demanding to speak with you."

Shit. I didn't have time for another emergency tonight. I had to get back to my apartment and come up with a plan. I couldn't stay in Denver anymore.

I nodded and started to push past her and out the door, but she stopped me with a hand on my arm. "Listen, June, I don't know what's going on, but I think you should hear this guy out. And you know, if you need anything, I'm here for you." Her chocolate brown eyes pleaded with me and I nodded again, slower this time.

"Ok Stacy. I'll see what he wants. Just please keep Jax and his new friends away from the alley until I figure it out."

Stacy smiled and gave me a quick hug before I stepped out into the crisp Denver night air.

And came face to face with Sheriff Joley.

7

CADE

The late summer sun beat down on me, as I flew down the mountain highway that led back into the city. The fields of wildflowers that dotted the vast expanse along the highway blurred by in a kaleidoscope of colors. I'd spent the past couple of months traveling all over the country, and had seen some beautiful places. But nothing compared to Wild.

Oranges, pinks, and purples melted into a waterfall of colors across the sky, as the sun sank behind the snow-peaked mountains. As the outskirts of the city appeared on the horizon, I felt a moment of nostalgia.

In the past five years, Wild had grown by leaps and bounds. Decades ago it had just been a small, wild-west city with more cowboys and miners than it knew what to do with. Over the years it had evolved, with ranches popping up along the outskirts, and the main city developing as a tourist attraction for people that wanted to get away, but couldn't quite afford the prices in some of the more high end resort areas like Aspen. Skiing wasn't as popular as hiking, mountain biking and other outdoor activities in Wild. But there was one main reason the city had grown so much over the decades, and that was all due to the bikers.

Motorcycle enthusiasts came to ride the winding, mountain roads and to take in the gorgeous views. Plus, it was a convenient stop between some of the bigger cities like Colorado Springs and Denver. It was one of the main reasons I'd decided to come back here in the first place. Growing up as the son of a prominent motorcycle gang member, I'd been around bikes my whole life. It was all I'd ever known, and I'd fallen in love with them.

After all that had happened, I never thought I'd want to come back to Wild again. I never thought I'd come back to any city for that matter, because I'd be spending the rest of my life in state prison for a crime I didn't commit. I waited for the burning rage to hit me, the feeling that had been a dark passenger with me since the night of my arrest, but nothing came.

Instead, there was peace.

Calm.

I smiled.

Looks like Mac had been right. The old biker had told me I would never appreciate where my life had brought me, until I got out and experienced some of what the world had to offer. My life had always been about bikes, the gang and trying to get my dad away from it. I'd never allowed myself to think outside of it, other than the times I'd spent with Juniper.

So I'd done just that. The custom motorcycle shop I owned was doing well with Mac managing it, and we had more business than ever. I'd spent every day since I'd been released from prison, working on building the clientele and reputation of B's Custom Creations, as one of the best custom bike shops in the state of Colorado. Probably on all of the West Coast, to be honest. I'd poured every ounce of blood, sweat, tears and rage I had into the place, trying to forget my childhood and my past. But once it was up and running, the rage remained.

I'd taken Mac's advice and left to see what the world had to offer. I'd spent the past few months visiting friends I'd made in the motorcycle world, both from my prison past, and my business. Then I'd culminated my trip with a final whirlwind party stop in Sturgis, the mecca of the biker world.

As the miles rolled beneath me, I felt the years I'd spent simmering in a pool of anger and rage slip away. The night of my arrest, I'd been so sure that Juniper would come bouncing into the Sheriff's station at any moment to give her statement. But all that had come was a letter from her father's law firm stating that Juniper Wild had no knowledge of my whereabouts on that night. The judge had taken one look at the last name on the company header, and with no other witnesses to testify on my behalf; it had been a slam-dunk case. They had offered me a plea deal if I agreed to give up any information on my dad, or his known associates. A deal I had refused to take.

So I'd been rushed through a sham of a hearing, and sentenced to the maximum allowable punishment for arson and attempted murder—up to forty-eight years in the slammer. I gripped the handlebars tighter as a wave of emotion overcame me. Not rage this time, but gratefulness. I'd been out for three years now and had only ended up serving two years total. Word had gotten around to some of the biker clubs that I hadn't snitched on my old man or his buddies, and eventually, that was rewarded with someone pulling some strings to get me an appeal. Once it was determined that I'd not been given a proper hearing or trial by my peers, the sentence was overturned and I was immediately released.

Sturgis had been exactly how I'd imagined it and I'd let myself experience everything it had to offer. I'd spent so much of my teen years chasing after my dad, trying to clean up the mess of his life, that I hadn't really paid attention to what other guys my age were doing. By the time my twenties rolled around, I'd been in the state penitentiary. Women had come and gone in my life since I had been released, but none had really grabbed my attention. None like Juniper.

I frowned at the thought. While the miles of open road had quieted the rage, the image of Juniper's pain-filled blue eyes never faded. It didn't matter that she had ruined my life. I didn't know how to convince my brain to just forget her. It helped that no one had seen or heard from her in over five years. The only connection she had left to this city was her father and brother, and the former seemed to prefer staying at his residence in Colorado Springs, rather than his family home in Wild, leaving his son to be cared for by their housekeeper.

I'd asked about Juniper, just once when I'd first gotten back to the city and had crossed paths with Edmund Wild. His cold and impassive face had seemed to harden, and for a moment, I thought he wouldn't answer me. But then, he just bit out a sharp, "She's doing exactly what she should be doing, and doesn't have any interest or time to deal with you." And then he'd gotten into his Mercedes and peeled away into the night.

The words had stung. Juniper had just left and never looked back. She'd truly turned into the Wild her father had always wanted her to be. She was probably living some high-society life with her arranged-marriage husband, not giving me a second thought. I resolved then and there to move on and forget her.

Moving on had been easy. I wasn't a bad-looking guy, once I'd gotten out of prison, my scars and tattoos seemed to only enhance women's interest in me. It had gotten worse after one of the major biker magazines picked up a story about a custom job I did, and I'd had my photograph taken. It wasn't by choice though. The photographer had just so happened to catch me on a particularly hot day, working on one of the bikes outside with my shirt off, and had decided to go with *that* for the cover story instead of the nice, professional-looking headshots I'd agreed to. By the time it was published, the damage was already done, and I'd earned the reputation as the local playboy, on-line fan club and all. Mac often grumbled about the number of ladies that would stop by the shop, or call unexpectedly to track me down, saying it was a distraction to the guys. "We're a bike shop, not a damn dating service!" He'd growl at me. It wasn't enough of a distraction for me though. I still couldn't forget *her*.

The city grew larger in the distance and I slowed down, my custom Indian Scout rumbling beneath me. The trip had been long and exhausting. I was looking forward to a hot shower, my bed, and maybe one of those *distractions* Mac complained about. But first, I needed to stop to grab some lunch and then check in on the shop. This had been the longest—outside of prison, that I'd been away from my tools and work. I was desperate to get back to the smell of motor oil and the rumble of a finely-tuned engine.

The original city of Wild still stood as a reminder to the past. A rustic jewel set in the sprawl of new, urban growth. It was just one of the contradictions that made Wild unique. Old Wild and New Wild set as a juxtaposition of each other. One pushing the new, out, preserving its history and tradition, or maybe keeping it from pressing in. As I passed by the mix of old, historic buildings, I felt something I hadn't felt since before the night my world had come crashing down. I felt light. I felt like I was home.

Pulling up to the curb outside of Katy's Diner, I glanced around at the unusual amount of work trucks and skilled laborers crossing the street, and noticed that repairs were being done to a string of old buildings that once housed a saloon, a sheriff's office, and a jail cell. It was left over from the days of old, where miners could get their fill of whiskey, be arrested for public intoxication, and then sleep it off in the jail, all in one go. I frowned as I noticed a sign being painted in bright, sunshine yellow with large, bold calligraphy above the buildings. *Wild's Emporium.*

It was then that I noticed a trio of women standing beneath the covered porch of the buildings, nodding their heads as they bent over what looked like a set of architectural plans. I let my gaze travel appreciatively over the one in the middle, who had her back turned to me. Speaking of distractions. My eyes were immediately drawn to the sweet curve of her ass and the way she filled out the denim jeans she was wearing. She was looking at the plans and speaking to who, I assumed, was the head of the construction crew. I could tell by the way she gestured, that something wasn't quite right, and she wasn't happy about it. She remained with her back to me, but the way she cocked her hip, then tossed her blonde hair over her shoulder, I could tell she wasn't going to take 'no' for an answer.

I wasn't sure what it was that drew me in, but I was like a moth to a flame. I told myself it was just curiosity and the need to move after sitting on my bike for so long, but the next thing I knew, my long legs were carrying me across the street to the little group. Not that I noticed anyone but the blonde firecracker who was now rolling up the drafts and tapping the poor foreman in the chest with them. I wanted, no, *needed*, to see her face. Something told me this was exactly the kind of distraction I was looking for, and I wasn't going to leave until I was sure she wasn't taken, and had my number programmed into her phone. The thought that she might not be single made me frown. I hadn't even seen her face yet, or knew her name, but the idea that she was someone else's, made my gut churn.

As I came closer, I could hear her speaking to the foreman, giving him hell. Her voice sounded just as sexy as the backside of her looked, and I found myself repeating a litany in my head. Words I hadn't used in years. "Turn around, pretty girl. Turn around. Let me see you."

Suddenly, either because she'd somehow heard me, or sensed me behind her, I saw her back stiffen, and she stopped waving the rolled-up plans in the man's face.

She turned, and it was like everything: every breath, every heartbeat, every thought, every minute, just stopped as twin pools of deep, blue eyes looked up and met mine.

Juniper Wild was home. And then, I saw black.

8

JUNIPER

*I* was standing on the raised sidewalk, left over from the days back when the city was still just a small, wild city and not because of its name. The historical buildings had been left pretty much intact for the better half of the century, so you could still walk the wooden sidewalk and steps that led to what had once been the heart of the city, the saloon. The construction manager winced as I shoved the plans he'd just handed to me, back at him. For the third time this week, we'd been delayed for the Grand Opening of Wild's Emporium, due to one of his crew members not showing up to work. I'd had enough.

"Dennis," I began.

"Darrel." He interjected.

"Right, Derrick." He gave me an exasperated look.

"I don't care who didn't show up, and what they have to do before we can pass inspections. I would suggest you figure out a way to get the job done." I tapped him again. "And if that means you need to strap on a tool belt and get your hands dirty, well guess what, D-man, you just gotta do what you gotta do. I am not delaying my opening again. And if I do? You're going to see the rest of your payment go up in the form of decorations and balloons. Do we—," I paused my tirade when I noticed that he wasn't looking at me, and kept glancing nervously over my shoulder. I looked at my two friends who were standing next to us, but weren't the least bit concerned with the conversation, and instead were *oohing* and *ahhing* over the new gas lamps that were getting installed outside of the entrance.

"Den— I mean, Darrel!" I snapped at him, and his eyes swung back to me. "Can we do that? Please?" I added the please as an afterthought. When the renovation company had first started on my new project, they'd been all "Yes, Miss Wild! Of course Miss Wild!" But I'd figured out quickly that they assumed that because I was a pretty face with a little bit of money, they could drag their feet on the work and try to squeeze a few extra bucks out of it.

Unfortunately for them, I'd had plenty of experience with maintenance and construction workers at The Pit, whenever we needed to do repairs or renovations. Also, unfortunately for poor Darrel, and the real reason that I kept forgetting his name, was that he was the third construction manager the company had sent to the job, after I'd refused to allow the last two to come back. I really didn't want to have to deal with a fourth, considering we were so close to completion, and Darrel really had been a decent manager. He just had shitty laborers.

I started to open up the plans to ask another question, when suddenly I felt a presence at my back, as a dark shadow fell over me, blocking out the sun. The hair on the back of my neck stood on-end and I stilled, as I could have sworn I heard a dark, rich voice rumble behind me. "Turn around, pretty girl." But it was so low and murmured so quietly, it might have just been the exhale of a breath. Still, whoever it was, was causing Darrel to not pay attention to what I was saying.

I turned around to deal with the new presence so I could get back to work, and felt the earth fall from beneath my feet.

Cade.

Only, it wasn't Cade. Not as the hazel-eyed boy that I remembered anyway. No, this version of Cade was bigger, harder, and darker in every way.

His sun-kissed brown hair was pulled back into a low bun at the nape of his neck, with wisps falling free from his temple, as if they were too wild to be tamed. His skin was several shades darker than I remembered, and the jaw that I'd once placed tender kisses along, had hardened into a knife's edge.

My eyes were drawn of their own accord to the shoulders that filled-out a dark gray cotton t-shirt, and hugged arms that looked like they could have split the seams with one, well-placed flex. Tattoos snaked up from his wrists and disappeared beneath his sleeves. Dark whorls of black ink and smoke, flames, skulls, and other things I couldn't quite make out. My artist's eye was immediately drawn to the quality of the line work, and the delicate way the black ink faded into gray.

And he was tall. Good Lord, he was tall. He'd always been taller than me, but I'd never paid attention to the height difference between us, but now, with him standing just a step below me on the porch of the emporium, and me in my heeled boots, he still towered over me. That explained why it had grown darker when he'd approached. He literally blocked out the sun.

Realizing that I was ogling his muscles, standing there like I'd forgotten how to speak, my eyes flew back to his face as I opened my mouth, but I choked on the words as something else caught my attention. An angry, puckered scar ran from the top of his left temple down across his face, just barely missing his eye. It stopped right before the Cupid's bow of his mouth. What should have been disfiguring, only made him look even more sinister and sexy, which had my heart racing in a way I hadn't felt in a long time. The magnetic pull of attraction surprised me. I hadn't expected to still feel it after all these years. It was nothing compared to the shock I felt when I finally dared to meet his gaze.

Rage. Glittering, black rage danced in his eyes.

My mouth went dry. Holy shit he was pissed.

When I'd arrived back in the city just a little over two months ago, I'd asked about him and hadn't liked the gossip I'd heard. Part of me had thought that maybe I could escape without seeing him again. The city had certainly grown up enough that we might not have even noticed each other. But there was another part of me, a secret thought that I tried to bury, that mourned the idea of not seeing him again. Maybe that made me even more of a coward.

His eyes burned into mine, sending thrills down to my core. I swallowed thickly. "Well, well, I should have known when I saw the sign. Just like a Wild to splash their name all over everything— even if it doesn't belong to them."

I flinched at the undertone of hatred and accusations in his words, and instantly went on the defensive. "Actually, Cade, this whole strip *does* belong to my family. It was deeded by the original city when it was founded." I crossed my arms and glared at him.

My statement only seemed to enrage him more, and a sneer curled the corner of his lip upward, highlighting the scar. It should have made him disfigured, but all it did was draw attention to the sharpness of his cheekbones.

"Deeded?" He snorted. "Figures. Everything just gets handed to a Wild, doesn't it? How long did it take for you to waltz into city and have everyone here rolling out the red carpet?"

I bristled more. He knew how much I hated the way this city fawned over my father and family.

"What's your problem Cade? I was minding my own business until you showed up."

"*My* problem?" His jaw flexed and his entire body seemed to vibrate as if he was barely containing himself. "*My* problem is that for five years, no one has heard from or seen you. And then one day, you show back up, claiming you own this property and business now. Where the fuck have you been Juniper?"

I flinched. This was not the conversation that I was prepared for or wanted to have with him. Especially with an audience. "What I was doing or where I was, is none of your concern." *You told me to leave.* I wanted to say, but held back.

"Oh that's right." He snarled. "I forgot, a Wild doesn't get questioned. A Wild doesn't have to explain themselves or their actions."

"Do you have something you want to get off your chest, Cade Black?" I snapped back, taking a step forward even though it meant that I had to crane my neck to look up at him. I'd run away from the fight five years ago, and part of me was still afraid of facing him, but I wasn't the same scared girl anymore. I'd faced-down more bullies and egotistical assholes that didn't know how to take 'no' for an answer, than I'd wanted to admit. I'd been ridiculously naïve about the world outside of Wild. But my eyes had been opened, and I knew a man who was pissing for a fight when I saw one.

We stood so close that our chests brushed against each other accidentally, sending a thrill of awareness through me. His very male scent of sun, leather and the open road filled my senses, and if it weren't for the pure rage that radiated off of him, I would have placed a hand on his muscled chest and breathed him in. I'd always loved the way he smelled after a long ride on the back of his bike. I took a step back to get control and refocus, but then I noticed the way he was staring at me. His gaze dipped down and I realized that from his vantage point, he had a clear shot down the front of my very thin tank top. I felt my body tighten deliciously in response to his gaze, and when he looked back up at me, there was a darker glint in his eyes, and he smirked as if he could sense what I was thinking.

"I don't think I'm the one that needs to get something off," his eyes dipped back down before he leaned in to murmur in my ear, darkly, and my pulse sped up again. "...their chest. Your daddy taught you how to use *all* your assets, well. Didn't he?"

Before I could register his statement or the innuendo, he'd turned around and was marching back across the street to his bike, then he was gone in a rumble of exhaust pipes and a cloud of dust.

I watched his retreating figure as he roared out of city with a mix of rage, guilt and something else I didn't want to acknowledge. Longing. I knew I'd have to face my past one day. I just didn't know it would hate me so much.

## 9

### JUNIPER

*I* stared at Cade's retreating figure as he drove toward the outskirts of the city. Whatever I'd imagined my first time seeing Cade again would be like, had been a far cry from what had just happened. It left me feeling hollow and empty, in a way I hadn't experienced in a long time. Not since my mother had died. And then, there was the undeniable attraction I still felt toward him. The magnetic pull of his presence was just as strong as it had been when I was eighteen, if not more so. All the tattoos and scars seemed to highlight the dark and dangerous side to him, that I'd only seen once before, on the night my father's schemes had brought my dreams of us being together, crashing down.

The memory of our last time together slammed into me. A vivid movie that played out in my head night, after night for months, even years after I'd left Wild. The way he'd trapped me against the barn pole. His rough hands like a hot brand on my skin. The feel of him filling me, the pain and pleasure. The punishment for my betrayal. The punishment I'd foolishly wanted, because I thought maybe it would atone for what I'd done. The release he'd denied me, and the cold way he'd dismissed me.

I'd seen the darkness he tried so hard to bury that night. A darkness that was entirely my fault for releasing. Or was it? Was this the real Cade? Had all of our time together been nothing but a silly, girlish fantasy?

"Ooof, looks like someone still has it bad for you."

A soft voice next to me startled me out of my thoughts, as I turned to face my friends who had been standing behind me the entire time. I'd almost forgotten they were there, or that I was in the middle of putting the last-minute touches on my new business venture, Wild's Emporium.

I looked at the two women, long-time friends from high school, arching a brow. "Exactly what part of that exchange makes you think Cade still has any feelings for me, other than pure hatred?"

Violet, a pretty brunette with curves for days and chocolate brown eyes, gave me a sympathetic look. "Honey. Cade's been back in city for all of about, three or four years, I'm not sure the exact amount of time, since I moved back after he did. And ever since that photo of him on the *HotWildRides* page went viral, he's gone through about half the female population here in Wild. And that's assuming the *tame* rumors are true. If that can't make a man forget why he's pissed at his ex-girlfriend, then nothing will. Are you ever going to tell us what happened between you two?"

I flinched. When the subject of Cade came up after I moved back home, I'd shut down every conversation. I didn't know how to explain to my friends what happened that night, or why I left. And I hadn't wanted to reveal my part in it. "It's old history and doesn't matter anymore. If Cade wants to play the part of fuck-boy and asshole, he's welcome to it. Just so long as he stays far away from me."

Lacey stepped up and put a hand on my arm, forcing me to look back at her. While Violet was all curves, Lacey was a willowy woman with a figure that should have been strutting down a runway as a high-fashion model. But she never seemed to notice or care for her appearance, or fashion and had fully embraced the hippy-eccentric vibe that permeated Colorado mountain citys. Right down to the beaded headband that encircled her honey blonde hair and the orange, paisley-print palazzo pants she'd paired with a multicolored crochet top, that I was sure she'd made herself. She shook her head, the colorful beads that dangled from her headband, dancing. "We just need to get you your own little group following so that you can move on too. You know what they say," her eyes danced and she gave me a wink. "The best way to get over a guy is to get under a new one. Maybe more than one."

My jaw dropped in shock and I couldn't help but snort with laughter. "Ok first of all, I don't need to get over Cade. I'm already over him, we are old history." One of her brows arched, and even Violet gave me a look that said she didn't believe me. "And secondly, I am not interested in dating, period. So there is no need to get under, or over, anyone." Lacy looked like she was about to argue, but then I noticed Darrel motioning me over to where he was standing, and I moved away, thankful that the conversation was cut short. I'd ignored the subject of what Cade had been up to for the past several years, for a reason. It was going to be hard enough knowing he was still in the same city, but knowing about his life? That would be torture.

Darrel grinned at me as if he'd just won the prize blue ribbon at the Fall Chili Cook-off. It was a much different attitude than the pessimistic and apologetic tone he'd had a few minutes ago.

"D-man, I hope by the way you're smiling at me, you've got some good news?" His toothy grin was endearing and soothed away some of the unease I was feeling, and I caught myself smiling softly back in return.

"Indeed, I do Miss Wild! Indeed, I do!" He waved a piece of paper in my face enthusiastically and I had to duck a bit to avoid getting smacked with it.

"What's this?" I eyed the flapping page suspiciously.

"This is what we've been waiting for!" He practically beamed with pride, but when I stared at him blankly, not understanding the unnecessary enthusiasm, he flipped the paper around so that I could read it clearly.

"It's the inspector's report. We passed!"

I looked at the paper with a bold, official-looking, signature at the bottom, then back to Darryl. "You mean, we're good? No more delays?"

Darryl nodded his head. "That's correct."

Suddenly my grin matched his and I turned around to my friends who were watching the exchange with rapt attention. This news meant so much for all of us.

"You hear that? Wild's Emporium is open for business!"

Violet squealed and clapped her hands, while Lacey let out an enthusiastic "Woo Hoo!!" and pumped her fist in the air. It had been a long couple months of uncertainty and stress while we waited for all the permits and construction to be done. So much was riding on the opening of the emporium, and its success. It was more than just a new business venture for the heiress to the Wild legacy. Not that there was much of an inheritance to speak of.

My friends leaned in to give me a congratulatory hug, and for a moment, I let the relief and joy wash over me before the weight of everything else in my life could overshadow it.

Pulling away, I took out my cell phone to shoot off a text to the other ladies, who were going to be relieved to hear that the emporium was going to be open soon. The returning *ding* of smiley faces, hearts, and excited dancing gifs, made me grin all over again. It felt good to feel like I was finally able to put my family's name and resources into something I believed in.

Tucking my phone back into my pocket, I turned back to Violet and Lacey who were busy discussing opening day plans and activities.

"Ok, I'm going to leave the party planning to you, ladies. I've got to get back home and check on Dean."

Violet glanced up at me, her brown eyes softening with worry and sadness. "How's he doing? Still not talking to you?"

I sighed and shook my head. "Nope. Well, yes. But only if you count one-word answers and grunts as talking."

Violet shook her head and gave my arm a squeeze. "Be patient with him, Juniper. He's been through a lot. My River was like that after her dad left. It didn't matter what I did or said. She was so hurt and angry, but she couldn't express it and instead lashed-out at me. Sometimes when someone is deeply hurt, they take it out on the people they love the most."

I sighed. "I get that Vi, I really do. I just wish he would do *something*. Yell at me. Tell me I'm the worst sister ever. Punch a wall!" I ran a frustrated hand through my long hair and shook my head. "Ok, maybe not that. We can't really afford to fix a hole in the wall at the moment. I just wish he would start to let some of what he's been bottling up, out, before he explodes and does some real damage. I can't help him if he won't *talk*."

Both ladies gave me sympathetic looks, and squeezed in hugs before I turned and jogged down the steps toward my parked car. If I'd thought dealing with Cade had been tough, he'd at least expressed his emotions and communicated very clearly how he felt about me. Dean, however, had only said one full sentence to me since I'd come back to Wild and had been appointed his guardian. "You should have never come back."

10

JUNIPER

Gravel crunched under my tires as I took the winding road that led up to our family home. The Wild's of generations before had been miners, ranchers, business owners, even bankers. When we'd first settled in this valley, it had been a Wild West city with every kind of outlaw and societal outcast, coming to a place where they felt they could escape their past. I wasn't quite sure if it was just a tall tale, exaggerated over years of retellings and embellishments, but it was rumored that my ancestor, Jesup Wild, had been a bank robber, and that somewhere in the mountains surrounding us, a hidden treasure awaited someone lucky enough to stumble upon it.

I snorted, thinking about the fabled "buried treasure". Wouldn't that just solve all my problems? When Sheriff Joley had shown up outside The Pit, it had been both a blessing and a curse. Turns out, I hadn't needed to be so worried about Jax spilling my secret after all. In his gruff way, Sheriff Joley informed me that Father had been in a single prop-engine plane crash on its way from Wild, back to Colorado Springs. There were no survivors.

Edmund Wild was dead.

Emotions bubbling up like a pot of water, just on the verge of boiling over, rushed through me. Confusion, anger, sadness, grief, and one I hadn't expected to ever feel, regret.

Numbness replaced all of them, however, because with his next breath, the sheriff was informing me that I was the heir to the Wild legacy, and sole guardian to my little brother, Dean. Then I was being driven back to my apartment, almost as if on autopilot, and the next thing I knew I was following the Sheriff on the long trip back to a place I'd never thought I'd see again. Home.

The house came into view, a white behemoth built in the days of Victorian gables and wrap-around porches. It was surrounded by the colorful wildflowers the city was known for, encased by green hedges and stone pathways. It wasn't lost on me that flowers meant to grow wild, were trapped in flower beds meant to contain and control their beauty. A sweeping lawn stopped at the edge of a cliff, overlooking the valley and the small, glittering city below. From the original edges of the city, you could look up at the mountain and see the lights of our house twinkling in the distance. One of the bankers in generations' past had decided that our family needed a family seat, as if having a whole city named after us wasn't enough, and had built the home with the idea that we'd someday court politicians and rich businessmen here. And we had, for a while. I remembered finding an old photo album in our attic, flipping through the black and white photos of women dressed in shimmering gowns and men in top hats and tailcoats. It had looked magical, and my curious brain had practically exploded with questions as I'd dragged the book down to my mother's bedroom to show her what I'd found.

I pulled into the circle drive and parked my VW right outside the main porch. Popping open the door, I hopped out to take the steps leading up to our front door, two at a time, wincing when I noticed that one of the boards had come loose again.

This great, big house had been built on the wealth of generations' past, and the legacy of our family name. A legacy that had been pounded into my head over and over again. A legacy that I was somehow supposed to uphold, honor, and dutifully take my place in the long line of Wild women who had come before me. A legacy, and fortune, that was now somehow squandered away, with a house that was falling down around me.

The irony was not lost on me. We'd gone from being supposed bank robbers to bankers, to now having the bank almost foreclose on our home.

I wondered if that was why my dad had stopped searching for me. He knew there was nothing left for me to come back to. And the threat of withholding his money would no longer mean anything once I learned there was nothing there but an empty bank vault, and piles and piles of debts and collection notices.

A small wave of guilt overcame me. What if I had stayed? What if I'd done what he asked? Could I have helped? Why hadn't he told me how bad things were? The what-if's circled my thoughts like vultures as I opened the oil-rubbed oak door, stepping into the cool interior of my childhood home.

It no longer felt like the prison of my youth, but the weight of the inheritance I'd been left with still surrounded me.

"Bess?" I called out as I set down my keys and purse on the entry table.

"In here June-bug!" A cheery voice answered me from the kitchen at the back of the house.

I took in a deep breath as a whiff of something sweet caught my attention and I grinned. Bess was baking scones again. The scent of lemon and sugar scattered all of the remaining dark thoughts and worries, as I made my way to our kitchen where a woman with silver hair and a kind smile, was busy rolling out and cutting dough on our large kitchen island. The kitchen had been the last thing updated in the home, courtesy of my mother, and boasted double ovens, a large, French stove with multiple gas burners, and all the counters and work space a chef could dream of. My mother had loved to bake and cook before she'd gotten too sick to do it herself, I had a few memories of sitting on the counter licking a spoon of chocolate frosting as she'd hummed and worked.

When Bess had come to us, she'd taken one look at the large kitchen and immediately started crying tears of joy. I think that was the reason my mother had hired her. She wasn't the traditional housekeeper or nanny my father had wanted to put in place to care for us. But she was kind and funny, and she loved to bake. My mother had seen a kindred spirit in her.

I snatched a freshly-glazed scone from the cooling rack and leaned against the counter to watch Bess work.

"We finally got the last permit and the inspection passed. Wild's Emporium will open in three days!" I grinned around a mouthful of lemony goodness.

Bess dropped her rolling pin and let out an enthusiastic "whoop!", her hands coming together for a loud clap, sending a cloud of flour into the air.

I laughed softly as I watched her break into a jig in the middle of my family's kitchen. Thank God for Bess. If it hadn't been for her joy and sometimes enthusiastic outbursts, life would have been even more miserable for me here in Wild.

Bess had been the one to *ooh* and *ahh* over my artwork. She'd been the one to celebrate when I'd earned enough money for my dream car. She'd been the one to hide my college acceptance letters from my father and had encouraged me unashamedly to step away from the family legacy and follow my own dreams.

"I know your mother June-bug. She wouldn't have wanted this life for you. Go explore and find out what the world is all about outside of your family name."

My mom and Bess had become good friends in the short time they'd spent together before her death. I would hear their laughter ring through the whole house as they regaled each other with tales from their youth. It was something that I was forever grateful for.

"Where's Dean? I want to share the news with him." I picked up another scone and went to the fridge for a glass of milk to wash it down.

Bess shook her head and went back to filling a pan with fresh-cut scones before popping them in the oven. "He's at school and won't be home until later if he's gone to the bike shop. Oh! That reminds me." She shut the oven door and went to a little writing desk, tucked away in the alcove of the kitchen. It contained a landline phone, some notepads, pens, and a few magazines Bess liked to keep around for reading. I'd tried for years to get her a cell phone, and had even recently bought her one, but she kept it tucked away in the drawer saying she preferred it when people couldn't reach her at all hours of the day. I wasn't sure she'd even turned it on.

She ripped off a piece of paper from her notepad

and handed it to me. "I got this voicemail from the school office saying that they needed you to call them. But then my first batch of scones didn't turn out right and I forgot to call you."

I took the paper and noted that she'd written "urgent" at the top and frowned. I loved Bess to death, but the only thing she ever found urgent was if her dough didn't rise properly. Glancing at the clock, I saw that there was still more than half the day left in the school day, and pulled out my cell phone to redial the number.

A woman answered after the third ring with a crisp "Principal Snyder, here, how many I help you?"

I had no idea that the number I'd dialed had been the principal's direct number. Or that it was the principal of the middle school I'd been directed to call. I stumbled through my words.

"Oh... umm... yes this is Juniper Wild. I was told someone from the school had called me. I'm sorry Principal Snyder I didn't know this was your number. I'll call back to the main office."

"No, Miss Wild, I'm glad you called. I was the one who left a message for you. I thought it would be better coming from me rather than someone else, considering the circumstances."

I frowned, she didn't sound like a principal

calling about trouble with a student. And yet, what other reason would she have to call?

"Is there something wrong? Is Dean ok?"

"Dean is fine." The woman hesitated. "However, the boy he punched is not. Now, I've managed to placate the boy's parents, for now—"

I interrupted her. "Excuse me? Dean *punched* someone?"

"Yes. He did, and as a result, per school policy, he has been temporarily suspended. Now, because of the circumstances, we aren't going to enact further punishment such as expulsion, even though with his record, he certainly would warrant consideration for it—"

"*Expulsion?!*" I interrupted her again and this time, Bess stopped rolling out her dough to come walking towards me, a concerned expression lined her face. "You mean to tell me that Dean has punched enough kids at that school that you're considering expelling him?"

"Miss Wild, I know that you've just taken over guardianship of your brother and you may not be aware of all the—, " she paused as if searching for the right word. "...*difficulties* that Dean has had over the past year. So that's why I think it would be a good idea if you could come in with Dean and we can discuss a course of action. Dean is a bright kid, and has a lot of potential, but you understand we can't have him influencing and distracting the other students with his negative behavior and outbursts."

I didn't know what to say. The thought of my sweet, baby brother punching or bullying anyone was so foreign to me that I almost laughed at the absurdity. But then it had been five years since I'd seen him. Five years for things to change. Five years for my father to dig into him and try to mold him into the man he thought he should be.

"Miss Wild. Do you understand? Miss Wild?" The principal's voice shook me from my thoughts.

"Yes. I understand Principal Snyder. Just tell me when and where, I'll be there. Thank you for calling." Then I hung up before she could give me a time and date. Her secretary could call me later if it was that important. But for right now, I didn't want to hear the principal's version of Dean's school history.

My brother had given me the silent treatment far too long. It was time for him to talk.

## 11

### CADE

She was back.

Juniper *fucking* Wild.

The darkness at the edge of my vision hadn't faded since I'd torn out of the city like I had demons chasing me. And they were. Nightmares of my past. Of the day she'd left and everything had come crashing down, replayed over and over in my head.

Those big, blue eyes staring up at me with so much hurt, so much pain as she'd lied to my face. Those same eyes stared at me all over again, taking in my scar, flinching in shock, and then hardening and giving me a look I'd seen all too often. The same look Edmund Wild had given me. Like she had a right to be there just because of who she was.

It didn't matter that I'd baited her. Didn't matter

that she'd been just as shocked to see me as I'd been to see her.

Fuck her for coming back and turning my whole life upside down again. Just when I thought I'd finally gotten it right.

My shop came into view. The large, white, metal building with its simple logo, a metal, all-black "B", "C" and "C" in a large circle, the only adornment above the glass front doors. I hadn't wanted to advertise my name too much because of my father's reputation, but something had prevented me from choosing anything other than my last name as the official legal name of the business. To everyone else, it was just "B's Custom Creations" and the logo stated enough. Just like the understated signage, I was content to take a back seat in the business operations. That's where Mac came in. He was the big, burly biker and face of the shop. My job was to create the dream motorcycles that our clients paid us big bucks for. Even if they didn't know what they wanted, I did. It was what I lived for. The only thing that had ever calmed the rage inside me. The only thing that had ever brought me peace.

The minute my hands touched a new bike, it spoke to me, and I'd get lost in bringing it to life.

Rows of bikes lined the front of the store. They

were all recent drop-offs from clients who were eager to have a one-of-a-kind motorcycle. Mac had told me that I'd have more than enough work to keep my head quiet, and he hadn't been lying. I eyed each one, the possibilities momentarily distracting me from my rage, but then a familiar dark blonde head appeared around the corner, and the anger rose to the surface again.

"What are you doing here, Dean?" I barked out the question harder than I should have, inwardly cursing at myself as I saw the kid flinch. *Fuck.* He didn't deserve my anger but something about seeing him after the showdown with his sister, set me on edge again. Dean shrugged, his face hardening a bit, then turned to look at the row of bikes.

"Got out of school early today, so I came here. I didn't know you were coming home today." He was lying. I knew him well enough now to know. His voice was still caught in that stage between boy and man, a little high-pitched, but he spoke so quietly that you almost couldn't hear him. It had taken me months to get him to open up to me when he'd first started coming around the shop. To be honest I wasn't sure at the time why I wanted him to talk at all. He was a Wild, and Juniper's brother. I shouldn't have wanted anything to do with him.

But he'd been so quiet. Just sat and observed while I worked or while the other mechanics talked about the bikes that were brought in. Only Mac had been able to get any kind of reaction out of him, a smile or a short laugh.

I'd found myself talking to him while he watched me. Not asking him any questions or even caring if he responded. The quiet was just unnerving for some reason. So I'd started talking about parts and mechanics, about aerodynamics and the way a bike would perform if we swapped out different parts. I'd mutter to myself and ask questions as I thought out loud and eventually, he started answering me back.

For a while, I could forget that he was Juniper's brother, and that he had the same last name as the man who'd ruined my life. He'd opened up and eventually became a stable-figure at the shop. Pestering me with questions, talking about bikes, and school. But never Juniper, and never his Dad. Once I'd asked him, casually, about his family and his sister.

I wasn't sure what had made me do it, other than morbid curiosity maybe. But he'd said nothing and then disappeared from the shop for a full week. Mac had threatened me, thinking I'd done or said something to the boy to hurt his feelings. But when he turned up seven days later, he hadn't said a word about my question, and I never asked again. We left it at that. In the shop, he wasn't a Wild. And I wasn't a man his family had ruined.

I crossed my arms and stared at the boy. Now that Juniper was back I could see the family resemblance. He was slightly built with dark blonde hair, just a shade darker than hers. They had the same blue eyes. The same slightly upturned nose. The same facial expression when they were lying.

"School just started and I know Principal Synder doesn't do half-days." I let my accusation hang in the air, but my eyes caught him shoving his hand deep into the pocket of his jeans. "Let me see your hand."

His jaw flexed stubbornly. Another similarity to Juniper that I'd forgotten about. After a brief stare down, he finally sighed and pulled it out to show me his swollen, scratched knuckles.

I frowned, examining the cuts and bruises. "You finish it?" It was all I asked. It was all that needed to be asked. While I may not have gotten much out of him about his home life, I knew one thing, his dad sure as hell wasn't going to teach him how to be a man or stand up for himself. And after a few instances where he'd shown up to the shop with a busted lip or bruised ribs, I'd waited until his wounds were healed, then took him out back and taught him how to defend himself. I wasn't the only one in city with a grudge against the Wilds, but I wasn't going to take it out on an innocent boy.

He nodded and pulled his hand back. "Yeah. But I'm probably going to get expelled for it. Snyder called my sister."

I flinched at the mention of his sister.

"Snyder's not going to expel you. I'll talk to her." I opened the door to the shop, knowing Dean would follow me, and headed past the small showroom where we displayed some examples of our work, to the back office where I kept a mini fridge and some ice packs. He'd come in with more than one bruised knuckle to make me keep them in stock.

"I wish she hadn't come back."

I stopped dead in my tracks, not sure if I'd heard him correctly. Not sure if I wanted to respond. But I couldn't help myself. I had to know.

"Why did she?"

Dean sighed and I caught a glimpse of him in one of the showroom mirrors. His face was sunken, cheeks hallowed and his eyes were distant and cold. It was the face of a boy haunted by nightmares. It was the face of a boy, of a man, I'd seen one too many times in the mirror, myself.

"Because my dad died."

I wasn't sure I could handle any more surprises in one day. Edmund Wild was dead? That's why Juniper came back?

"I'm sorry." I wasn't. Edmund Wild wasn't a loss anyone in society would mourn, except maybe the cutthroats and murderers he protected. I opened the door to the office and flicked on the light switch.

As if by somehow muttering the words, a weight was lifted from his shoulders, he plopped down on the faux leather couch across from my desk and shook his head. "Don't be."

Again an unsettling feeling of déjà vu danced across my skin as I glanced at the kid. There was a hauntedness to his expression, but there, in the glimmer of his eyes, was also a small flicker of relief. I knew that feeling. How many times had I wished for my dad to disappear? To be gone from my life for good, just so that I didn't have to deal with the fallout from being his kid? The sins of the father weren't an easy burden to carry. But when he'd finally passed away from liver failure after a life of drugs, alcohol, and hard riding, it wasn't grief I'd felt. It was relief. And then guilt for feeling that way.

"So your sister is taking care of you now?" I opened the freezer door and pulled out an ice pack and tossed it to him. He caught it and dutifully placed it on his hand, not flinching when the cold made contact with his skin. It was another lesson I taught him. Never start a fight, always finish it, and never let them see you hurt.

Dean shrugged as he held the ice pack in his hand. "I guess. I wish she'd just stayed gone."

*Me too.* I leaned against the desk and crossed my arms over my chest. My stomach growled and I cursed. I'd stopped in city to get food and had been distracted by Juniper. She hadn't been back in my life more than a couple hours and she was already wreaking havoc.

I pulled open a desk drawer where I usually had a few protein bars stashed, and tossed one to Dean before tearing open my own. Dean snatched it out of the air with his good hand and ripped open the package with his teeth, biting a huge chunk out of it. "So, you'll really talk to her for me?" he asked around a mouth full of protein bar.

I frowned. Dean's sister was back. She should be the one talking to Principal Snyder, but I'd handled more than one altercation for Dean, and knew the principal would listen to me.

"Yeah, I'll talk to the principal for you."

Dean shook his head. "No, not her. My sister. I need you to talk to Juniper and tell her."

"Tell me what?" I flinched as a voice I had never wanted to hear again, much less two times in one day, filled my ears.

Dean's head snapped toward the door at the same time mine did.

Juniper stood there, her arms crossed under her chest, her hip cocked out in the sassy way that told me she was on edge. I hadn't paid much attention to what she looked like outside of the old buildings she was renovating, other than when I'd been admiring the way her ass filled-out her jeans. But I could see more, now that the rage had died down. Her honey-blonde hair hung in soft waves around her shoulders, longer than I remembered. The thin, black tank top that she'd tucked into the top of her jeans, hugged breasts that were mouthwateringly full. The image of how they'd looked peeking over the top of her bra when I'd glanced down her shirt earlier, made my cock harden. For the first time, I noticed how her face had matured, losing some of the softness, but her lips were still full and pouty. And pressed into a thin line of rage. I stopped my assessment and met blue eyes that were blazing with suspicion and anger, as she looked between me and Dean.

Those gorgeous eyes that were like an electrical

current straight to my cock narrowed as she stepped into the room. Seeing her in city had been one thing. Seeing her in my shop, however, made the fact that she was back, a cold dose of reality. Five years of nothing. Five years of rage. Five years of never knowing the answer to the question, *why had she done it?* Why had she betrayed me?

"Why is my brother here with you, Cade, instead of at school where he belongs?" She looked at Dean, sitting down on the couch with an icepack on his knuckles "And why is my brother getting threatened with expulsion from school?"

Why do I want to kick her brother out, grab her by the neck and kiss her until she tells me the damn truth this time?

## 12

JUNIPER

The last place I'd ever expected to find my brother, was with Cade Black.

When I'd checked all the places I thought a preteen boy might go to hide out, he'd been mysteriously missing. After remembering that Bess had mentioned he went to a bike shop after school sometimes, I'd pulled up his phone location that I'd forced him to share with me, and followed it, only to end up at a completely different kind of bike shop than I'd pictured. This wasn't the store in city that sold normal bicycles and catered to the road bikers and tourists. No, this was a bonafide motorcycle shop unlike anything I'd seen before in Wild. The simple logo above the door didn't give me any clue as to the name or who owned it, but I instantly knew this was the shop my friends kept referring to, and who it was that worked here. And apparently my brother had been hanging out with him for years.

I seethed.

Any lingering thought I had that maybe Cade just needed some time to process my return home, vanished when I saw how his gaze hardened, and nearly every muscle in his body tensed the minute I walked into the room. I had to stop this foolish hoping and wishing that we could put aside our history The Cade and Juniper of the past were gone and done.

A bridge burned.

I'd given him the match. He'd doused it in gasoline and lit the bitch up with a smile.

"You need to start talking." I bit the words out and saw Cade open his mouth to speak, so I cut him off. "Not you. Him." I turned to my brother. "What are you doing here, Dean? What happened at school today?"

Dean glared at me in stoned silence. Great. Another guy who hated my guts.

"Dean, go home. We can finish our talk tomorrow." At Cade's order, my brother rose, and I felt my anger rising with him.

"Sit back down. You're not going anywhere until

I get some answers." Dean paused, the snap of my voice surprising him. He'd never heard that tone with me before. He looked back at Cade questioningly, and I seethed. Would he really listen to Cade over me? I turned back to Cade. "Just what exactly are you planning to talk to Dean about tomorrow? Why is he even here?"

Cade ignored me and instead nodded to Dean. "Go on Dean. I'll handle this."

Before I could protest further, Dean scrambled past me and was out the door. But I saw the look of relief on his face, and something in my heart shattered. How could my own brother despise me so much? What had I done? But then I knew the answer, and guilt gripped my heart.

I turned back to Cade, my jaw clenched so tightly that I could feel the vein pulsing in my temple, feeling the first tinge of a world-class migraine coming on. "What the fuck is my brother doing here with you?"

Cade leaned against the desk and crossed his thick arms over his muscled chest. The office wasn't large, just big enough to hold a large desk, the couch Dean had been sitting on, and a small refrigerator. The walls were painted a muted gray, along one side were posters of custom bikes. It looked like they had taken the photos outside of the shop. On the other wall was a large cork board with more photos and postcards pinned to it. Cade's smiling face was in several photos as he posed with girls wearing barely-there tops and short-shorts hanging onto him with love-sick expressions. His fan club. A flare of jealousy rose, and I had to quickly squash it. It had been five years, and the man hated my guts. Technically, I should hate him just as much for what he did to me, too. Gripping tight to the memory of how he'd left me on the barn floor, after I'd given him everything, including my innocence. I moved further into the room to face him.

Darkness danced in his gaze. "Maybe you should ask your brother that."

I gritted my teeth, my temple throbbing harder. "I would, but I'm more likely to squeeze water from a rock than get an answer out of him. He hasn't exactly been open with me since I came back."

Cade shrugged, "Not my problem."

God, this man was infuriating. "Well, it seems to be your problem, since you were so willing to help him out just a few minutes ago. How long has he been coming here?"

"Dean's business is his own, and if he wants to tell you, he will. I'm not going to force him."

Black spots danced in front of my vision. I had to get out of here before the migraine fully descended on me, and I was puking my guts out on the side of the road, unable to see or drive.

"Fine. Don't tell me anything. But do this, stay away from my brother. Obviously, whatever influence you've had on him hasn't been a good one since he's being threatened with *expulsion.*"

Cade snorted and pushed away from the desk. Even with the short distance between us, his presence was overpowering.

"Let's get something straight. Things have changed since you left, Juniper. Just because your last name used to be *Wild* doesn't mean you get to waltz into my shop and tell me what to do like you own the place. You don't own me, Juniper. You never have, and you never will."

I raised my chin a notch, hearing the challenge in his voice and rising to it. "My last name is still *Wild* but you're right. A lot has changed since I left. The Cade I knew would never influence or encourage a little boy to fight. I'm giving you one warning. Stay away from my brother."

He closed in on me, and damn if the way he stalked towards me didn't light up some dark part of my soul. Every nerve in my body vibrated with his nearness, even as I felt the barely-contained rage radiating off him in waves.

A dark gleam flashed in his eyes. "Still a Wild? Interesting. I'll make you a deal, pretty girl." His voice was a dark whisper. It curled around me and I leaned towards him just to hear what he was saying.

"What deal?" I eyed him cautiously, trying to determine what his next move might be. What could Cade possibly want to bargain with me for?

"The truth. You tell me why you're really back in city and I'll tell my boys to run Dean off the next time he comes around the shop." He towered over me and once again I was struck by the height of him. He'd make Jax look like a gnat.

"My dad died and I'm now Dean's guardian. There, now leave him alone." I spun away, but he caught my arm, whirling me around so fast I couldn't see straight. My head throbbed and nausea threatened to bubble up the remains of my lunch. He stopped me just as I felt the edge of his desk at my back, and I gripped the cold wood to steady myself. I closed my eyes to fight through the wave of nausea and when I opened them again, found myself staring directly into glittering, hazel eyes. He'd trapped me against his desk, preventing me from moving.

"You might be a spoiled, little rich girl, Juniper,

but you're a terrible liar." His eyes narrowed as he watched me lick my dry lips, then dragged them slowly down the length of my body. I sucked in a breath of embarrassment at the way my nipples pebbled, and the way my body responded to his gaze. He met my eyes again with a knowing smirk, as if he could sense what he was doing to me. "What happened to the fiancé? Did he bore you? Run out of money? Or maybe it was something else."

My eyes widened. "Fiancé?" I croaked out in confusion. "What are you talking about?"

He either hadn't heard me or had chosen to ignore what I'd said and continued on, moving in closer to me, one jean-clad thigh sliding between my legs until I was half-balanced between his leg and the desk. His lips grazed the side of my neck as he spoke, just barely dragging them against my skin until I was shivering against him.

"Poor, little bird in her big house, with her fancy dinners and luxury cars, bored and alone. Daddy dies, and now you can swoop in and play the grand heiress to the Wild legacy. And while you're at it, maybe have a little fun on the side?" The friction from his leg between my thighs was torture as heat and moisture pooled there. Whatever my mind was trying to convince me about Cade, my body was disagreeing wholeheartedly. It didn't matter that this Cade was a complete asshole, I wanted him just as much now, as I did when I was eighteen. Possibly more. His knee pressed harder into my core and I moaned. There was no way he couldn't feel how wet I was through my jeans.

"I"m only here because my dad died and my brother needed me." I panted, my hips grinding myself against his leg all on their own, even though I wanted to resist. But then I'd never been able to resist Cade Black, and wasn't sure that I ever could.

"I don't think I believe you, pretty girl." He leaned in and I closed my eyes as I felt his breath against my cheek.

"What do you mean?" My mind was mush. The throbbing pain had dulled to a low ache behind my eyes, as every other nerve ending was on fire from his nearness, his words, his touch. One hand slid under my tank top, barely skimming my ribs and stomach, the other reached up and grabbed a fistful of my hair, yanking my head back so that my body arched against him. His head bent, lips grazing over the tops of my breasts.

"I think you're here to finish what you started all those years ago." His tongue lazed a slow path from the top of my breasts to the hollow of my throat.

How had this happened so fast? How had he managed to switch me from being a justifiably angry sister, to nearly orgasming on his desk? The friction from his leg against my core built, until I was a gasping, grinding mess on his thigh, and my heart slammed the door shut on those thoughts. Screw the how or why. This is what I needed and had wanted for years.

"You're right about something. The Cade you knew would never have done this." His teeth nipped against my sensitive flesh and his husky voice whispered in my ear. "Are you coming on my thigh, pretty girl? Tell me, when he fucked you, did you scream my name?"

The memory of the barn came crashing down and my eyes flew open. The next thing I knew, my palm landed a sharp *smack* against his cheek and he pulled back, a snarl on his lips.

"I don't scream, think, or even spend a fraction of a second on *anything* that has to do with you, Cade Black." I disentangled myself from between his legs and the desk, making my way to the door. "Stay away from my brother. Or so help me God, I will end you. That's a promise."

I didn't wait to hear or see his response and walked out of the door to the office, past a wide-eyed receptionist who looked like she was trying hard not to listen in on our conversation. I hoped she hadn't had a view of what had just happened either. The last thing I needed with Wild's Emporium Grand Opening, was any gossip or rumors starting about me or my family. It was going to be hard enough to drum up business as it was. It wasn't like I had a six pack and alpha-hole attitude to bring the women clients flocking to me.

A sudden thought made me pause at her desk. "Excuse me, do you have a business card?"

The receptionist, a middle-aged woman with victory-roll styled hair that was colored to match her bright, red lips, stared at me for a moment before smiling. "Why yes, of course!"

I matched her smile. "Great! And does it have the owner's number on it?"

She glanced at the office behind me and then gave me a curious expression. "Well, yes, but are you sure you'll need it?"

I thought for a second and then shook my head. "No, you're right. I don't want to bother the owner. I'm sure they're busy. What about the general manager? Does he have a card?"

The women looked at me, baffled, but pulled out a white business card and handed it to me. I gave her another polite smile and hurried out of the building before my migraine got any worse.

Cade was right. I didn't own him. I didn't want to own him. But if my family name had any influence in this city at all, I'd use it to do everything I could to protect my little brother. Even if that meant keeping friends close and enemies even closer. And if it got me a little payback while I was at it? Even better.

I grinned as I walked back to where I'd parked my car but it dissolved into a frown. I'd been so furious at him, and my reaction to him, that his words hadn't even registered. Cade thought I had a fiancé?

But then I didn't have time to think about it anymore as the only thing I could focus on for the next few minutes was making it home and to my bed.

## 13

### JUNIPER

My eyes opened to a pitch-black room.

It wasn't alarming, though. By the time I'd made it home from the motorcycle shop, my migraine had been in full force. Pain radiated in waves from the top of my skull down to my neck. The late afternoon sunlight drove knives into my eyeballs, and I was nearly in tears by the time I reached my front door. I didn't even bother to look for Dean, just noted his bicycle leaning against the fence, and then headed inside, going straight to my room.

Bess came in a few minutes later, took one look at me, drew my blackout curtains shut, and placed my migraine medicine and a glass of water next to my bed. I mumbled an incoherent word of *thanks*, downed the meds, and immediately passed out.

Normally, I'd sleep through the night and into the next day, depending on how long the migraine lasted. But something had sent all of my senses on high-alert, pulling me from my medication-induced slumber.

I lay there in the dark, the headache a dull, but manageable throbbing in the back of my skull, and listened.

The house was perfectly quiet. I could hear the *tick* of an old grandfather clock in my father's old study, just down the hall from my room, and the normal sounds of a house that was almost a hundred years old. No other noise stood out to me, and I drifted back to sleep, but then, there it was again. A soft creak, so small and quiet I almost thought I'd imagined hearing it. But it didn't come from inside the house. It was directly outside my bedroom window.

I was fully awake now.

Throwing back the covers, I approached the curtained window and pulled back the edge of the thick fabric, peering out into the darkness. Moonlight faintly illuminated the garden outside my window, and just beyond it, the greenhouse and shed where we kept our lawn tools. My eyes were still blurry from the medication and I had to blink a few times, but then I saw it. The door to the shed was open, and the light was on. The door that was shut and locked every night, ever since a few teens had decided they'd wanted to steal some of our lawn equipment a few weeks back.

I swore softly under my breath and quickly reached for a sweatshirt to pull over my head, as I left my room and made my way to the back hall that would lead to a side entrance door, and directly to the garden. The Colorado night air was just chilly enough that I could see my breath, misting out before me. Apprehension was replaced with anger as I stomped across the garden path to the shed. I would have a talk with Sheriff Joley in the morning about these teenagers. I couldn't afford to keep replacing yard tools every time some kids wanted to dare each other to do dumb shit.

Speeding up, hoping maybe I'd be able to catch them before they could leave, I reached the open door and flung it open, wider. But it was empty.

I stopped and stared at the shed. Nothing was disturbed. Not a single tool was out of place. I picked up a gas can and shook it, thinking maybe they'd gotten a free gallon or two out of me. But it was just as full as it had been the other day. Confused, I reached for the string hanging from the single, swaying light bulb in the center of the shed to turn off the light, then let out a gasp of surprise as I saw it. There, on the back of the shed wall, in dripping, red paint, was a small, grinning skull, engulfed in a crown of flames.

Icy dread filled me as I stared at the grinning skull and it stared back at me. I knew that mark, and I knew exactly where I'd seen it before. And while I didn't know who had left it, I knew what it was. A threat and a promise.

Someone had marked me.

Sweat dripped down my brow as I stared at the grotesque image. I couldn't pull my gaze away. A thousand thoughts threatened to overwhelm me.

And then one thought above them all. Dean. I had to protect Dean. Panic, fear and adrenaline burst through me, and the next thing I knew, I was sprinting back to the house, screaming his name into the chilly night air.

I burst through the back entrance of the house and ran down the hall to the main staircase. Bess came stumbling from her room just off the kitchen, her white nightcap slid to the side and her fuzzy bathrobe open and dragging behind her.

"June? What's wrong? What's happened?"

"Dean! Where is he, Bess? Did he come home yesterday?" I didn't wait for her answer as I took the stairs, two at a time to the second level of the house, where the rest of the bedrooms were. Guilt that my migraine had incapacitated me so much that I couldn't check on him, made me choke up with emotion. If something had happened to him because I wasn't able to protect him... I let the thought trail off. Now was not the time to panic. He had to be in his room.

"Well, I believe so. I thought I saw him sneak in and grab a sandwich." Her voice huffed behind me as she tried to keep up with me, as I hit the top of the stairs and raced down the hall to his room.

"Did he leave again? Is he here now?" I didn't wait for an answer and hit his door, locked. "Dean! Dean, are you in there?" I pounded my fist on the door and shook the knob. I looked over at Bess, who was watching me with wide eyes, clutching her robe to her chest now. "Do we have a key?"

Bess shook her head. "I think there's a master key in your father's study. I'll go get it, but Juniper, what is this about? Should I call the Sheriff?"

"NO!" I shouted and wiggled the doorknob again, pounding on it louder. "I mean, yes, go get the key, but no, do not call the Sheriff. At least, not yet." Fear and dread left a sick feeling in my stomach. If I was marked, there was nothing that the Sheriff could do about it. And considering my father's previous business associates, I wasn't sure I wanted the sheriff involved in anything at all.

Bess nodded and hurried away to head back down to the main floor where my father's study was. I tried the knob again and pounded on the door once more. Just as I was about to shout his name again, the door swung open and a surly teenage boy stared at me. Dark blond hair stood on end all over his head, except for a few longer pieces that fell in front of his sleepy, blue eyes.

"What the fuck, Juniper? It's like 3:00am or something." He grumbled and rubbed his eyes.

"Oh, thank God." I was so overcome with relief that I didn't even bother to reprimand him for his language and grabbed him, pulling him into me. His thin body stiffened in surprise and I thought for a moment he was going to push me away, but as if he could sense my fear, he relaxed and let me hold him for the briefest of moments. Then the moment was over and he pulled away.

"What's going on Juney?" He frowned and looked at me and then at Bess as she was coming back down the hall, the master keys on a key ring in her hand.

I stepped past him and into his room, heading straight for the double windows that overlooked the front drive. This had been my room before I'd moved away, and when I'd left, Dean had taken it over. But I knew this room inside and out, which meant that I knew every way a teenager with a plan could get in and out without being detected.

Giving a quick three bangs to the windowsill, I slid open the old window with ease to Dean's startled "Hey! What are you doing?" and then swung my legs over and dropped the short distance to the second gable of our roof. Dean stuck his head out after me. "Are you nuts? What the hell are you doing in my room at 3:00am acting like a crazy person?"

I ignored him, and with the moonlight illuminating the rooftop and Dean's windows; I scanned every section, looking for evidence that someone had tried to get to him. But there was nothing I could see. Just Dean's angry face glaring at me from within his room.

Sighing, I turned in a slow circle on the rooftop, taking in everything that could be seen from this vantage point. The mountain peaks were shadows in the distance and I stopped to stare at them. Their inky darkness absorbed the moonlight as if they were an infinite blank space where no light could penetrate. The eerie sense that they were watching me, observing everything that was happening below their majestic presence, filled me and I shuddered.

Turning back to Dean's window, I gripped the windowsill and pulled myself up with a huff. It had been easier to do when I was seventeen. Sliding back through the window, I stood up and faced a furious-looking teenager with his arms crossed over his chest and no signs of Bess. She must have gone back down to bed. With his eyes narrowed and his lips pressed into a thin, disapproving line, I couldn't help but see how much he looked like our father. Anger flared. Had my dad done this? Had he put us in danger?

"You're switching rooms tomorrow." I dusted my dirty hands off on my pajama shorts, then shut the windows behind me, making sure they were good and sealed.

"Umm, no, I'm not." I turned back around, a brow arching at his words. Tonight had been the most Dean had spoken to me in months. Granted, it was because I'd busted into his room in the middle of the night like a lunatic. But, nevertheless, it was something.

"Yes. You are. I'm not in the mood to argue." And I really wasn't.

Dean threw his hands up in the air. "Oh, so you think just because you're in charge now you can come into my room, mess up my shit, act like a crazy person and I just have to listen to you?"

"Well, yes, actually, as your guardian, I *can* do just that." I crossed my arms, mimicking his earlier pose. "I lived in this room way before you did, D. I'm not stupid. You weren't in bed asleep the whole night and I know it."

He glared at me. "You're insane Juniper. I had no idea those windows opened up, or that you had a trick until now. So yeah, thanks for telling me that."

"Oh yeah? Then why did I find this out on the rooftop?" I pulled out a gray wallet and flipped it open, Dean's school identification glinting in the lamplight.

His eyes widened in surprise for a brief second, and then narrowed in a spiteful glare, shooting daggers at me.

When he said nothing, I sighed and closed my eyes, pinching the bridge of my nose. "Look, Dean, I get it. I was a teenager once too. And I promise I'm not doing this to punish you. I'm trying to keep you safe. Especially with this expulsion hanging over your head. The last thing you need or want is a reason for Snyder to follow through on it, and I haven't even had the meeting with her yet." I brought my hand down and looked at him again. He was studying me, wariness, and something else in his gaze. But he still didn't speak.

"So for me, just for a little while, can you please move your room? Until all this blows over?" I tossed the wallet on his bed in a show of good faith, and tried to give him a reassuring smile. He glanced at the wallet and then back at me before turning away completely. Dismissing me.

My jaw clenched, and I resisted the urge to force him to talk to me. I knew first hand how ineffective it was, and how much he'd just dig into his silence even more. I left the room, closing the door behind me. It may have been easier to just tell him the truth, that he was possibly in danger, but until I knew more, I didn't want to scare him. Seeing his wallet under his window on the roof had been the perfect opportunity, and I'd seized it.

When I made it down the stairs and turned down the hall to head to my room, I stopped as I came to my father's study. Normally it was kept locked up tight, but Bess must have left the wide doors open in her rush to grab the master keys. I peered into a room that was dimly-lit by one lamp on his desk.

I hadn't entered this room or even opened the doors since the day I'd been read his Will, and was declared the sole heir. The heir to nothing but debts and pain. The heir to secrets and lies. The heir to a legacy that had been left to crumble into dust.

I grabbed the doors and slammed them close, then hit the electronic keypad on the outside that locked the door. Whatever secrets my father's study held, I wanted nothing to do with them. They needed to die, just like he had.

## 14

### CADE

Hard rock music played over the speaker in the mechanic bay, and intertwined with the sound of mechanics laughing, talking shop, and revving engines. I was only half paying attention to the commotion around me as the new custom bike I was working on, was currently in pieces before me. A puzzle that was waiting for me to solve.

This beauty was a classic cafe racer. The client had brought it in after finding it at an online marketplace being sold for parts, and wanted it restored to its former glory. I'd convinced him that I could do that, and more. Now I was taking it apart piece-by-piece to see what was salvageable and what parts I'd need in order to bring it back to life.

A familiar voice sounded behind me. "Is that a Honda CB550?"

I grabbed a towel to wipe the grease off my hands as I turned to answer him. "Close, it's actually a CB750. More horsepower, a little heavier frame." I reached my hand out with a grin. "What brings the great Kage Diovolo out to my neck of the woods? Finally, decide to let me work on that wheelbarrow you call a bike?" The man clasped my hand with an answering grin. "Had a few days with nothing to do and decided to slum it." He cocked his head, dark eyes glittering.

Despite being in a three-piece business suit, I knew that Kage Diovolo was more at home right here in a grungy mechanic's bay, than in a boardroom. From his Italian leather boots to the top of his slicked-back hair, he was in all-black. His signature look. A single gold earring dangled from his left ear, a tiny pitch fork. No rings or adornments on his hands, just the inky black of skulls and flames that danced along the back of his knuckles. Some were grinning, some were crying, others had their jaws unhinged in screams of horror. All were burning.

I wondered for a moment what Juniper would think of the way the tattoo artist had depicted the images of the skulls. And then, just as quickly shoved the thought away. I'd found myself doing that more often than I'd wanted to admit since she'd left my office the other day. Part of me had been so sure she'd show back up at the shop and demand more information on her brother. The other part of me was glad that she hadn't. Just one day in her presence and I'd lost complete control. I had both the urge to strangle her and fuck her until she was senseless all at once. It wasn't like me, and until I could control myself and my actions around her, I wanted to stay as far away as possible.

I carefully cleaned and placed my wrenches back in my toolbox, before shoving it closed and motioned towards the front of the shop where the door to the showroom and my office were located. "Somehow I doubt you're here just for a friendly visit, as much as I wish it were true. You still owe me for that one bar incident in Sturgis, what was her name again?" Kage tipped his head back and laughed before clapping me on the shoulder as I steered him towards the door. "Yeah, sorry about that buddy. She was just too D*elicious*, for a country bumpkin like you to appreciate thoroughly." I snorted. "Well, she was appreciating me just fine until you walked in. But it's alright, the scene was getting too wild for my tastes anyway."

Kage gave me a predatory grin as we entered my office and I shut the door. "Ahh yes, I forgot you were still determined to keep up your 'good boy' image."

I grinned back and waved my hand at the wall of photos of fans from the magazine article, as I sat down behind my desk. "Not entirely a 'good boy'."

It was Kage's turn to snort as he took a seat across from me on the couch, one leg draped lazily across his other knee. Kage was nearly as tall as me and he dwarfed the couch. Yet his demeanor and the way he casually lounged on the faux leather, he might as well have been the one behind the desk. It was just in his nature. Kage Diovolo dominated whatever space he entered, and either you bowed to him, or you got out of his way. Friend or not.

"If you want to shed some of that 'good boy' image, Cade, you could have just said so. You know the offer still stands."

"To work for you?" I shook my head. "Sorry bro, the response is still the same. I'm happy here with my shop. I saw where that train led and I'm not interested in riding it."

Kages' dark eyes grew serious, but the smile still stayed in place. "Careful now, Cade. That train ride helped get you to where you are now. You wouldn't want to insult the conductor now, would you?"

Suspicion began to gnaw at me and I leaned forward. "That was pretty bold of you Kage. You just let your hand show, are you starting to slip up there, old man?" Kage was hardly old, but it was a long-standing joke between us, that the few months he had on me in age, made *him* my elder. The history between us was a long and complicated one. And while we'd both come from similar backgrounds, we'd each gone down a different path.

Kage grinned, humor leaking back into the pits of black as if he remembered he was talking to a friend and not an opponent. "Hardly, but I will get to the point, because I'm short on time and need to get back to Denver. I need you to keep an eye on someone for me and get some information from them."

I arched one eyebrow in curiosity. "Okay. You know I don't run in those circles anymore, you sure one of the boys in city can't help you?"

Kage shook his head. "No man. This one is a special case. I had a close eye on her for awhile, but then she managed to give me the slip."

I laughed and shook my head. "Seriously? *She?*

The great Kage Diovolo let a woman give him the slip? How many times did she turn you down?"

Kage shrugged. "What can I say? I got complacent. She hadn't made a move in almost five years and I had her right where I needed her until the time was right. Then one day I'm getting a phone call that one of my bars looks like a blood bath, and I've got some low-level punk from The Infernos asking for damages because she punctured his balls with a bottle opener." Kage was grinning, his eyes dancing as if he had enjoyed hearing about all the chaos the she-devil had caused. "Anyways, by the time I figured out she'd taken off and where I realized she'd headed, it was too late to stop her. I've had someone here keeping tabs on her, but I have some things in the works and need all my resources pulled back home." He cocked his head, leveling me with that black gaze and suddenly the suspicion from earlier turned into a gnawing chasm in my gut.

"No." I growled the word and Kage's eyes flashed soulless as he uncrossed his legs and leaned forward.

"Before you say another word, I think you should remember who's the conductor on your train." The smile remained in place, his gold earring with the pitchfork winking in the light.

"Fuck." I stood up from my chair and leaned

forward on my desk. "You can't make me do this Kage. This is not in our agreement."

"Agreements are dictated by the person who owns the contract. And I own yours Cade Black. Until the last penny is paid. I own it all." He sat back, draping a leg over his knee once more in casual confidence. His fingers tapped out a rhythm on his leg, the skulls on his knuckles grinning and screaming with the movement.

"Why her? Why Juniper?"

"You know the history of this city, right? How the Wild's founded it generations ago?"

I stood, stubbornly refusing to sit and give him the edge. Kage may have owned my contract, but he didn't own me. "Yeah, everyone knows how the Wilds' founded this city. It's on every damn street sign and poster."

"History has a funny way of twisting and distorting the truth. The history of Wild and it's founding, isn't as cut and dry as you think. You know how crooked Edmund Wild's dad was?" I nodded, anger still riding me. "Well he looks like a choir boy compared to some of their ancestors. Ancestors that made deals that are long-overdue to be collected."

I glared at him. "You didn't need to come all the

way from Denver to lecture me on how fucked up the Wild family is. You know that I've seen it up close and personal. But Juniper is one woman. The rest of the family is dead, other than her brother. Whatever you were hoping to get out of them, you're too late." A protectiveness rose up in me. As much as I hated Juniper, the idea that Kage wanted her for his schemes didn't sit right with me. The fact that he'd had someone in the city watching her and she hadn't been aware, made me want to punch the asshole, friend or not, in the face.

Kage cocked his head, a smirk curling at the corner of his lips. "Tell me something, Cade, you've been around the business enough to know this. Would a man like Edmund Wild, with all his secrets and all his connections, just let the family legacy die out with him? Or do you think he'd have a plan in place?"

I crossed my arms, resisting the urge to walk around the desk and drag him outside. Kage came from a world of violence and death. Just like I had. And while I'd worked to get away from it, Kage had embraced it, fully, by sinking down into the dark depths of that world, then rising to the top as king. Whatever he wanted with Juniper, I was sure that it was less to do with the woman, and more to do with her dad, and until I found out what it was, I had to tread carefully.

"You don't want Juniper. You want her dad." I probed carefully, unsure how far the safety of our friendship would go with him. "But why? What did Edmund Wild do to you?"

Kage shook his head and gave me a grim smile. "Tsk, tsk, Cade. You know better than to ask questions you don't want the answer to. As much as I'd love to welcome you back into our fold, I'm trying to keep you from hopping back on the train you despise so much. Or..." one dark brow arched sinisterly. "...I could find someone else, someone less-likely to be careful with her like I know you'll be."

I glared at him, rage seething. He knew he had me. He knew I wouldn't be able to resist the lure of finding out what secrets Edmund Wild had taken to his grave. And he knew that as much as I hated the woman for what she'd done, I'd never put her in harm's way. Fucking bastard.

"How do you expect me to get any information out of her? We don't exactly have the best history and I've made it pretty well known how much I hated her dad." I thought back to her, how she'd felt when I'd pinned her to my desk, her sexy body and little moans practically begging me to bend her over and take her right there. I hadn't known what came over me, or why I'd pushed and teased her that way. Just that once I'd touched her, smelled her, tasted the salt on her skin, it was like we were right back to being teenagers again, and I forgot that I hated her. Until she'd remembered where she was and who she was with, and had come at me like a raging kitten.

He shrugged, nonchalantly, as if my concerns were insignificant. "For now, just keep tabs on her. You were close once, get close again. Tell me if anything suspicious happens." He stood up, and I moved around the desk to stand in front of him. "Do this for me, Cade, and I'll consider your contract good. We'll be finished." He held out his hand, and I stared at it.

Juniper Wild was back in my life for less than a week, and already my world was turning upside down. Spying on her for Kage wouldn't get rid of her. But it would get me the revenge I craved for what her father did to me all those years ago. It would also answer the questions that had burned like a hole in my heart and soul for the past five years. Plus, I'd be free from my debt to Kage, and could finally sever the last tie of that life. Besides, it was better that I did it than some thug Kage would surely sick on her. With me, she'd at least be safer. I may be a bastard, but I'd never truly hurt her.

I gripped his hand and shook it.

"Deal. I'll be your inside man. But regardless of whether she tells me anything, or it leads to any information, we're done. My debt is paid."

We stared at each other, eye-to-eye, for a moment as our hands gripped. I knew it was a risk, changing the deal. Kage wasn't a man who left a bargaining chip on the table, and my contract to him was far from paid in full. He could have easily pushed for more, and he knew it. But for some reason, he just nodded and shook my hand. "Agreed. No matter what information you get or don't get, your debt is paid. Black's Custom Creations is yours, free and clear."

A weight like a boulder lifted from my shoulders, and I grinned.

All the pain. The time in prison. All the sacrifices I'd had to make. Watching my dad spiral out of control for all those years. It was worth it. I'd made our dreams come true. And all I had to do in return, was betray the woman who had betrayed me.

All I had to do was lie.

## 15

### JUNIPER

Just a few days after our building passed inspections, Wild's Emporium was open for business. I stood just inside the building, grinning at the sight of the balloons and streamers highlighting the "Grand Opening" sign. People were lined up and down the faux street, waiting for a chance to get in to one of the shops inside. There was a festive feeling in the air, and I was excited to check on the ladies who were running their stores. They were the reason this Grand Opening meant so much. Not because it was another business with my family's last name attached to it, but because it was the start of something fresh and new for each of us.

The emporium was set up as a small set of

boutiques and shops, each with their unique features and stalls. One was a bakery owned by Violet. Another was a crystal and reiki healing shop owned by Lacey. There were others in there as well, clothing boutiques, custom furniture and antiques, candles and pottery. All made, owned and operated by one of the women from this city. Women who had struggled to stand on their own. Women who were crying out for a way to make it in a world that had beaten them down, but not defeated them.

Part of the agreement of the emporium was that each shop would contribute to the upkeep of the facility, but no rent was owed. Instead, part of the proceeds from their businesses would go to women and children in need, a fund we named "The Wild One's Foundation."

My shop was here too. I didn't want to be seen as just the owner of the property. A property, in all honesty, I hadn't felt like I deserved to own. But if it was going to be mine because of some antiquated laws, then I was going to use it for something other than benefiting my family name. So in the very back of the emporium, in a place that was all my own, was a tattoo shop. It was something I'd been secretly working on for years. With all the influence of the bikers around me, and the ink I'd seen adorning their skin, I'd learned to appreciate the artistry and tradition of tattoo. But if I was being honest, it had all started with Cade. I used to keep a small notebook of doodles and ideas that he would share with me, for tattoos he wanted. After I'd left Wild, I'd taken to filling the pages with more drawings and ideas every time I'd thought about him. Soon, it had become an obsession, and had taken over my other art.

In Denver I'd become friends with an old artist who hadn't minded me pestering him with questions, and apprenticing under the table. It was a mutually beneficial relationship. He needed someone with younger eyes to do the intricate drawings that more clients were requesting, and I received all the training and knowledge his decades in the business brought. I'd enjoyed it because it allowed me to pursue my art in a different medium, but I had never gone further with it out of fear. It would have meant that I needed to register and jump through all the hoops to be certified. But now that I didn't need to hide who I was anymore, I'd busted my butt the past couple of months to clear the paperwork, and now I was a bonafide tattoo artist with my own shop.

It wasn't the art studio and gallery that I'd once

dreamed of, but that dream didn't even come close to the satisfaction I felt from having a client walk in and choose one of my pieces to be permanently inked on their body. It was a humbling experience I never tired of.

I wove my way through the crowd, stopping for a brief few moments to hug the smiling faces of the women working their cash registers and selling their wares. I grinned at Lacey who had set up a small table outside her shop, and had a line for tarot card readings.

"I thought you were saving the card readings for the auction?" I watched her long fingers shuffle the cards with the skill of a Vegas showman. She smiled and shook her head, her fringe dancing. "I am! But I decided they needed a little taste of what they're getting beforehand." She winked at a group of teen girls, who were giggling as they approached her table. "Something to sweeten the pot with." She glanced up at me and flipped the cards over, one dancing over the back of her knuckles as if it had legs of its own. "How's the special auction item going? Are we millionaires yet?"

I laughed,"Hardly, but it's going great so far. I can't believe women are actually bidding!"

"Well what did you expect? You're waving a giant

hunk of sex on a motorcycle in their faces. Of course they're going to open up their wallets for a chance. By the way, how did you get him to agree to it? I thought he hated you." A breathless voice and the scent of chocolate reached me. I turned to see a frazzled-looking Violet standing next to us with a tray of sample cupcakes.

"I didn't ask him, I asked his boss and he said he'd handle it. Vi, you're supposed to be selling your cupcakes, not giving them away." I looked back and forth between the two women. "You guys do know that this is supposed to be a business, right?"

Violet grinned and handed a cupcake to a smiling couple, that had just come out of a homemade soaps and candles shop owned by another friend of ours. The wife took a bite, her eyes lighting up in delight and immediately dragged her husband towards Violet's booth.

"You asked his boss?" Vi looked at me with a slight frown and then back at Lacey who was in the middle of explaining one of the cards to a curious teen, but before she could say another word, more customers had surrounded her tray and she was caught up in a conversation about custom cake orders. Backing away, I snagged a cupcake off her tray as I headed towards my shop, moaning in delight when the dark chocolate goodness coated my tongue. The emporium was designed to look like an old-fashioned market. The main path or street was made out of real cobblestone. The shop buildings all had faux gas lanterns that gave the illusion of flickering flames, and Victorian signage. We hadn't wasted a single ounce of space, and the emporium took up the entire length of a city block. When people walked inside, we'd wanted them to feel like they were stepping back in time.

Weaving my way through the crowd, I finally found my shop and stopped short at the figure who was leaning against the door, waiting for me.

*Cade.*

My heart stuttered and for half-a-second, I considered turning around and ducking into one of the other stores to check on the owner there, but then realized he'd already seen me and would know I was avoiding him. Instead, I raised my chin up a notch and approached him.

"What are you doing here, Cade?"

He looked up at the shop sign, "Juniper's Tattoo's", and then back down at me. "You're a tattoo artist now?"

"That's what the sign says. You didn't answer my question. What are you doing here?" I crossed my arms and glared at him. People were standing outside the faux windows of my shop where I'd put small samples of my work up for display. They were quick, little drawings that clients could pick from, called 'flash' that wouldn't take me long to turn out. I'd designed and drawn each one of them myself.

"I'm here because you wanted to speak to the owner of B's Custom Creation's." He moved away from the door and I unlocked it to enter the shop. It was small, with just one leather chair for clients to sit, and a work table for all my tools and ink. I could have opted for one of the bigger stores, but this one had something the others didn't, and selfishly, I'd taken it. Natural light from the only windows that faced outside the emporium, streamed in, illuminating my work space. My artist soul hadn't been able to resist its lure.

"I already spoke with the owner." I flicked on the switches that would power up my machines, and began to carefully lay out the sterile, packaged tools of my trade.

"No, you spoke with the general manager, Mac. You haven't spoken with the owner yet." He leaned casually against the door frame that separated the small waiting area, from my main work area, crossing his arms.

I slammed a drawer to my kit closed, a modified mechanics tool box, and turned around to glare at him. "What do you mean I spoke with the general manager? Isn't that you?"

He shook his head, a few locks of his dark brown hair falling into his eyes, and smirked.

Understanding dawned. "Fuck. 'B's Custom Creations. *Black's* Custom Creations. You're the owner." I was going to kill Lacey and Violet for this slip in communication.

The smirk widened, crinkling the scar at his lip and deepening the dimples in his cheeks. "Bingo."

My palms were suddenly sweaty with nervousness as I realized that my plan was about to majorly backfire.

"Listen, I know you're probably pissed, but the cause is a good one."

"Tell me exactly how auctioning me off for a date, benefits any cause other than your own personal agenda?" His voice was laced with accusations.

I winced. He had me there.

"It's not exactly a date. It's more like a personal experience." My explanation sounded lame even to my ears.

He arched a brow and held up his phone to read from it. "Explore the beautiful countryside surrounding Wild, Colorado with a one-of-a-kind experience. Enjoy the sweeping mountain vistas on the back of a custom bike provided by B's Custom Creations"'s, with Wild native and eligible bachelor, Cade Black. Picnic experience provided by Wild's Emporium." Hazel eyes pierced mine. "I wasn't sure who to be more pissed at, you for attempting this, or Mac for agreeing to go along with it."

"Oh please, we both know that if anyone else had suggested it you would have jumped at the opportunity. I did some asking around and it seems you have your own personal fan club, Mr. Black. I'm just capitalizing on an opportunity to drum up business for a good cause." I crossed my arms and leaned against my workbench, mimicking his stance.

When I'd first contacted Mac, it had been to request a donation for our charity auction benefiting The Wild One's Foundation. He'd been stand-offish with me at first, thinking that I was another heartbroken girl trying to get to Cade. Apparently the showdown the receptionist had witnessed at the shop, hadn't done me any favors either.

It had been Mac's suggestion that I make the auction more enticing since it was difficult to find someone to donate a bike, or anything else on such short notice. Then, when I'd jokingly suggested auctioning off a romantic countryside ride to appeal to the women's market, he'd loved the idea, saying he thought it would be a great way to get a little payback for all the hell Cade's love life had caused him. When I'd worried about getting him to agree, Mac had just laughed and said not to worry about it. No man could resist being the object of so many women's affections and attention. He'd make sure Cade went along with it.

"How much money has been raised so far?"

It wasn't the question I expected him to ask.

"Umm, for the whole auction? Almost ten thousand dollars." Inwardly I squirmed. Canceling Cade's portion of the auction and losing that money would be a major blow to the foundation. The other auction items were bringing in good money, but the Wild Ride experience was the biggest earner, by far.

"Who is the highest bidder?" His face was unreadable and I fidgeted from one foot to the next.

"I'm not sure, it's a blind auction and we won't see names until it's closed, but I think the highest amount so far is a thousand dollars." Had I felt a little bit of jealousy when I saw the bids start pouring in online? Maybe. But I sure as hell wasn't going to admit it.

He nodded and then without another word,

turned around and strode to the door of my shop. I called out after him. "You should be thanking me you know! I just cemented your place as Wild's most eligible bachelor!"

I watched as his tall figure retreated away from me. "Fuck."

What was I going to do if he refused to go through with it? Why did I secretly hope he would?

16

JUNIPER

*A*fter the fifth unanswered call to Mac, I'd finally given up, deciding if I only had one more day to live before being mobbed by a crowd of angry women, then I was going to spend it doing what I loved.

Wiping away the soap off the skin of my last client, I held up a mirror for them to admire their new ink. She'd asked for a simple outline of books and flowers in the short time we had, and would come back later for the color. I was already envisioning how I'd shade the flowers to cast shadows, and how I'd use various techniques to make the pages look like they were moving, as if by magic.

The bell to my shop jingled merrily, and I almost called out that I was closed, but then noticed it was

Lacey. I motioned for her to wait a moment as I finished up with the client, giving them instructions on their after care and scheduling their next session.

Lacey peeked at the girl's tattoo and whistled. "Woah girl. I knew you were always good at art, but I didn't realize you were *this* good. That's beautiful!"

I smiled and began to clean up my tools and area. "Thanks! I never thought I'd be into tattooing, but there's just something about it. It's like I'm creating living art and I love seeing how happy a client is when I'm able to bring their visions to life."

Lacey waited until the client left before she rushed forward and shoved her phone in my face.

"Tell me you saw it! Oh my God, please say you saw it." Her eyes danced with excitement and she practically vibrated with energy, the metal bracelets on her arm tinkling as she shook her phone.

"Umm, ok Lacey— first of all, how many of Vi's cupcake samples did you take? And secondly, no I did not see anything." I tried to step around her but she just sighed, rolled her eyes and slapped her phone into my palm.

"Just look!"

I glanced down at the screen, my jaw dropping in

shock. It had to be an error. I refreshed the page and then sank down into one of the waiting area chairs as the number didn't change.

"Someone bid ten thousand dollars on Cade." My voice was a shaky whisper. It was the highest bid received, and with the numbers from the other auctions coming in, had bumped our total amount to close to twenty-thousand dollars. That amount of money would be more than enough to get our foundation going. But who would bid such a high amount?

"Not just someone. You. You bid ten thousand dollars on Cade." Lacey's statement shocked me more than the number on the screen.

"What! That's impossible! I don't even have ten pennies to rub together, much less ten *thousand* dollars." I held her phone back out to her. "There's got to be a mistake. I need to announce that Cade is not in the running for the auction too. He figured it out and paid me a visit." I stood up and grabbed my jacket, heading for the door. I was already dismissing the numbers as fake, and mentally preparing myself for the announcement. A sudden thought gripped me. "Oh! And thanks a lot for not telling me that *he* is the owner of the bike shop. I felt like an absolute idiot for not realizing it."

Lacey looked at me, her brows furrowed in confusion. "Juniper, how could you not know? It says it in the name! "Black's Custom Creations."

I opened the door of my shop and scoffed as I waved my hand at the nearly empty emporium, as most of the customers and shop owners had made their way outside to hear who the winners of the auction were. The faux gas lamps flickered in the dark, making it look like it was truly nighttime inside. In a few hours, the cleaning crew would come through and sweep up the debris and trash, and reset everything for the morning. "Because I've been a little busy maybe? And you guys just kept referring to it as 'the shop'. You never once said he owned it."

She shook her head and followed me out, as we made our way down the corridor that acted as a street, and towards the entrance. "Ok that's fair, but I really don't think this is a scam. The auction is closed. The bid came in at the last minute as a blind donation, with a note that said if it was the highest, then the prize should be awarded to you."

I frowned and stepped out into the cool, Colorado evening air. The temperatures were getting lower and lower as we headed further into fall. Soon, the first bits of frost from winter would start to appear in the mornings, and snow would begin accumulating on the mountains. This was one of my favorite times of the year in Wild, where everything seemed to be caught in a hushed state of waiting for the season to change.

There was a crowd gathered outside the emporium and someone had set up a microphone and podium. Nerves gripped my stomach as I approached it. Public speaking wasn't exactly my forte and now that I'd have to announce that the biggest auction item was off the market, I was looking forward to it even less.

I looked out in the crowd, hoping to see a tall figure there, but all I could see were the smiling faces of some very hopeful looking women. I groaned. This was not how I envisioned the first day going.

"Umm...hey everybody. I'm Juniper Wild." My voice shook as I started out, the mic screeching with feedback, and I winced.

"Thank you so much for coming out to celebrate The Wild Emporium's Grand Opening." I started to smile, then someone from the crowd called out.

"Just tell us who won the Wild Ride!"

I zeroed in on the voice, my eyes meeting a pretty

girl with teal colored hair and piercings in her brows.

"Well, here's the thing. Unfortunately it seems that the Wild Ride auction...." I was cut off as a rich, baritone sounded from behind me, and suddenly I felt a warm hand slip under my jacket and around my waist. I stiffened with the contact knowing exactly who it was that touched me.

"It seems the Wild Ride auction was won by none other than a member of our famous founding family. Juniper Wild."

I looked up at Cade, my jaw dropping in shock. "I absolutely did not—" but my words were ripped away from me again as a mixture of *boo's* and applause sounded from the crowd, drowning out my protest.

"I knew it was rigged!" An angry voice rose above the crowd, and I looked down to see a frowning blonde-haired woman in leather pants and a cutoff t-shirt that barely contained a set of breasts I was, quite honestly, impressed with. "No one but a Wild had the kind of money to out-bid all of us!"

I blinked. Us? And that's when I noticed that the shirt she wore had the logo to the bike shop on it, and in hideous sequined font, the words "Black's Wild Rider's" scrawled right across her chest. The angry looking women who were surrounding her, were similarly dressed with varying degrees of biker-chic attire and I suddenly realized what she meant.

"Wait you're the ones who put in the thousand dollar bid? Can you explain to me how all of you planned to ride on *one* bike?" I was dumbfounded.

The woman tipped her chin, giving the appearance that she was looking down at me, even though I was standing on a small platform above her. She crossed her arms, forcing her breasts up even higher somehow, so that it looked like her chin was actually resting on them. I wondered if she'd ever accidentally knocked herself in the face with them. "Humph, that is none of your concern. We pooled our money and placed our bid. No one else in this city could have beaten us unless it was rigged. By *you*."

"I didn't place a bid!" I was indignant and turned to Cade, glaring at him and hissed. "*You* did this. Explain to them what happened. I can't have the whole city thinking I rigged something just because my name is Wild."

Cade gave me a slow, lazy smile and my insides tightened, his hands gripped my hips and pulled me closer but it was to the crowd that he spoke.

"Now now. I'm just as surprised as you all to see

that the head of the auction won the grand prize. But who can blame her?" His fingers found their way under my shirt, tracing the curve of my waist and moved higher to my ribcage. I sucked in a breath, frozen in shock, and my skin burned where his fingers touched. "Plus, it's for a good cause right? And so long as the money is put towards the new charity, I'm happy to go along with it. Besides," he winked at chin-tit lady and gave her a slow once over that I was sure would leave her in a puddle right there in the middle of the street, "...you're welcome at the shop any time, Jessica."

That seemed to placate her, and while she still shot daggers at me, she and her posse of biker women moved away from the front of the crowd. Cade pulled me away from the podium and I allowed him to, so that the other owners of the stores could announce their own auction winners and prizes. When we were a safe distance away from prying eyes and ears, I rounded on him.

"What the fuck was that about?"

One brow arched at me as he leaned in, crowding my space. "That, pretty girl, is called you-reap-what-you-sow. You put me in an embarrassing position without my knowledge or permission. So I did the same to you."

I seethed. "I put you in a position you were already gunning for. All the women in this city practically throw themselves at your feet and the ones that don't are either too young, or too old. Besides, it was Mac that said you'd go along with it."

Cade crossed his arms and grinned down at me. "Women throw themselves at me, huh? Why does it sound like little Miss Juniper is jealous?"

I sniffed. "I am absolutely not jealous." Jessica's chin-tits and the way she'd leered at Cade flashed in my mind. Ok maybe I was a little jealous. "If you want to get even with anyone it should be Mac. He led me to believe *he* was the owner, and that you'd love the idea. Said it was basically every red-blooded males dream come true."

Cade closed in on me, his fingers gripping my chin, tipping my face up so that I couldn't look away from him. His voice practically growled it was pitched so low, and at the sound, heat shot straight through to my core. "Oh trust me, Juniper Wild, I'm going to get my revenge on Mac. But first, I'm going to get what I'm owed."

I blinked. Dazed and captivated by the way his hazel eyes flashed with gold. My own eyes zeroed in on his lips. "Owed? I don't owe you anything, Cade." I breathed.

His grin was dark and full of promise. "Ah but that's where you're wrong, pretty girl. I won that bid in your name. And the bid was for a Wild Ride. I plan to collect it."

He dropped my chin and I gaped at him. "You can't be serious!" I sputtered as he began to walk away.

"Oh I am dead serious Juniper Wild. You owe me. In more ways than one. I'll let you know when I intend to collect." He didn't look back as he made his way to a group of men, leaning against their motorcycles. One of them glanced up at me, a smirk dancing across his lips, and something gold flashed on his ear. A moment of familiarity struck me, but then Lacey and Violet were surrounding me, having just picked their auction winners.

Violet grabbed my arm and looked in the direction I was staring, watching as one-by-one, the men started their bikes and pulled out into the street. Cade and the man with the gold earring were the last to leave, both of them staring in our direction until the last possible second. It was Violet who spoke first, her voice sounding shaky.

"What did Cade want?"

I swallowed. "Revenge."

"And the man with him?" I glanced at her,

frowning at the concern I saw in her eyes. "I'm not sure. Are you ok Vi?"

She nodded. "Yeah, it's nothing. He was just in my store earlier." She looked at me and smiled, the worry and concern fading away. "Ten thousand dollars for revenge, huh? That's a pretty hefty price tag."

I sighed, watching the bikers' retreating backs. "Yeah. One I'm not sure I can pay."

17

JUNIPER

It was the weekend, and the first time I was going out in ages. After Cade had roared away with his biker buddies, I hadn't seen or heard from him in almost three days. I'd spent the next twenty-four hours waiting for him to call, or to show up at my shop to demand his repayment, flinching every time the bell on my door chimed, or my phone rang. But he never did.

On the second day, I'd become angry. I wasn't a toy he could just pick up and play with any time he chose. Yeah, we had a fucked up past and relationship, but we were adults now. It was time to handle things like adults and discuss our issues maturely. I said just as much around a mouthful of devil's food cupcakes covered in decadent chocolate ganache, as I leaned against Violet's bakery kitchen counter on the third day.

She gave me a side-eyed stare, then shook her head, pulling a fresh batch of cupcakes from the oven and popping in two more. "Juniper, how do you expect to have a mature conversation with a man you constantly think about getting down and dirty with? Not to mention, *you* were the one who entered him in a bachelor auction after dry-humping him on his desk. Maybe *you're* the one who needs to be more adult-like?" She slammed another cupcake tray down on the counter and began to fill it with more batter, a tiny frown furrowing her pretty face.

Violet was the more serious one out of our group of friends. But she hadn't always been that way. She'd been both studious, and outgoing. Captain of the Cheer Squad and the Academic Bowl in high school. Always up for a party and good time, but ready to pull an all-night study session before our finals. Like me, she'd grown up sheltered by Wild, and had longed to leave and explore on her own. A year older than me, she'd graduated and left for college before the rest of us. No one had heard from her in several years, until one day she'd shown back up with no degree, no job, and a toddler in tow. Now, as a single mom, Violet seemed to carry the weight of the world on her shoulders.

"Vi, are you ok?" I asked gently, watching as she meticulously poured and measured more ingredients into her mixing bowl, before locking it into place and turning it on. She sighed, her shoulders slumping a little and then turned back to me.

"Yeah, I'm fine Juniper. I'm just a little overwhelmed right now. I have a big order to get out and I still need to restock the store counters. Plus, River has been begging me to take her to see the newest princess movie. I've just got a lot on my mind." She smiled, but it didn't quite reach her soft, brown eyes.

"Is there anything I can do to help?" I was worried about Violet. She never seemed to take any time for herself, and was constantly consumed by what she needed to do next. As if there was a checklist in her head that only got longer and longer each day. She was just one of the reasons why I wanted the emporium to be successful. So that one day, hopefully, Violet could take some time away and do something for herself.

She laughed and shook her head. "Umm, absolutely not. You are a *terror* in the kitchen Juniper Wild. You are not allowed to touch anything."

A sing-song voice came from behind me. "Oh, are we discussing Juniper's culinary skills again?"

I glared at Lacey as she came around the corner with another friend, Janelle, right behind her. Janelle's wide, green eyes sparkled. "Do you remember the time she almost burned down the whole school in home economics class, trying to make a lava cake?" Her full lips split into a grin as she came to stand next to me, snagging a cupcake off a tray on the counter. Janelle was another one of the emporium's shop owners, although her store was a little more like an office than a storefront. As an interior designer, she kept samples and some statement pieces from showrooms there, but didn't actually have items to sell. Technically, Janelle didn't really *need* a storefront, or the emporium to run her business. She'd already made a name for herself in Colorado Springs, and was considered an in-demand designer. But when she'd heard about our plans and the foundation, she'd immediately contacted me to set up a branch of her office here in Wild, and I loved her even more for it.

I rolled my eyes. "It was one lava cake! And that oven was ancient. It was on its last leg."

Janelle nudged me as she licked chocolate off her finger tips. "Yeah, the leg you kicked."

I laughed and turned back to Violet. "Seriously Violet, you're flying round like you've got the devil on your tail. Are you sure you don't need any help?"

A look of pure panic flashed across Violet's face, so fast that, for a moment, I thought I was imagining things, then she shook her head and smiled. "No, I'm good. I just need to finish up these last few batches and pop them in the fridge. I'll frost the rest tomorrow and come in a little earlier to restock. You girls go enjoy your night."

Lacey came around the counter to give her a hug. "Are you sure you can't meet us? Even for one drink?"

She shook her head again. "I'm sorry girls, I really wish I could, but this order is massive, and I need all my babysitter hours if I'm going to fill it."

I looked at the racks of cupcakes that were cooling on her counter and once again wished that Violet would let us help so she could take some time for herself. But I knew she'd never let that happen.

With hugs good-bye, we headed out.

After the stress of the past couple of months, dealing with my father's affairs after his death, and the struggle to get the emporium launched, I was looking forward to letting loose.

The bar we chose was located in the new, urban expansion of the city. Wild had changed a lot since I'd left with bigger buildings and more nightlife going up, every day it seemed. Tourism seemed to be at an all-time high. And while I was glad to see it grow and change, proving that it could move away from the past, I still loved the original touches and how it embraced its history.

We walked inside and headed straight to a booth where drinks and a round of shots were ordered. Raising our glasses up, Lacey called out for a toast. "Alright ladies, here's to the first week of Wild's Emporium! Cheers!"

Glasses clinked and the liquid burn of straight tequila flowed down my throat. I sputtered. "Oh God, who ordered this?"

Janelle grinned and raised her glass up. "Bottoms up, buttercup! I thought you were some hard-ass, biker bartender?"

I laughed, feeling the immediate effects of the alcohol hit my system. "I was, but it doesn't mean I drink like one!"

The DJ started up, and the sounds of a 90's boy band filled the bar. With a shriek of joy, Lacey pulled us out onto the dance floor. It was one of the reasons we'd picked this place. They had themed nights, and tonight just happened to be dedicated to the 90's.

Time flew as we danced, drank and laughed in a carefree way I had not done in a long time. Part of me missed Stacy, wishing she could be here with us. I knew she'd have loved meeting my friends, and I vowed that after the weekend, I was going to reach out and see if she would come for a visit.

Declaring that I needed a break and wanted to get another drink, the girls followed me back to our booth where we slid into our seats, giggling.

Lacey leaned over and whisper-yelled into my ear. "Psst, June! Did you see the way that guy was staring at your ass?"

I sipped on my water and followed the direction she was pointing, seeing a handsome man leaning against one of the bars that surrounded the main dance floor. He made eye contact with me and raised his glass, then leaned down and whispered something into a passing waitress's ear who looked over at our table and smiled. Seconds later she was approaching our booth with a tray full of shots that she set down in front of us.

"From a friend!" She winked and whisked our empty glasses away.

Janelle whistled, "Well, now it looks like we need to be saying cheers to Juniper and her fabulous ass!"

I laughed and raised my drink in the air. "I'm sure he's just buying drinks for pretty girls." I winked. "But my ass *is* fabulous."

Lacey nudged me, her eyes wide and sparkling. "Well, miss *fine ass*, I'm pretty sure the only drinks he is buying are for you, because he's headed this way. Which is fine as long as he keeps them coming."

I looked up to see the man standing next to our table, a hopeful smile on his face. Offering a polite smile back, I raised up my drink. "Thank you for the drinks! You didn't have to do that."

His eyes twinkled. "Well, I'd say that I was just being polite, but I'd be lying. I was hoping it would buy me a chance at a dance."

I laughed, deciding that I liked his boldness. At least he was honest about his intentions. "I do believe it does, mister..." I trailed off, my brow arched as I gave him a slow once over, not at all trying to hide what I was doing. Was I flirting? Yes.Was I a little buzzed? Also yes. Was this man in any way, shape or form as attractive as Cade? No, he wasn't. But Violet's words about how I behaved with him had been swirling around in my brain all evening, and I realized she was right. I was never going to be able to act normal around Cade, so long as I was still hung up on him like a lovesick teenager. I had to move on, and for good this time. Not that I would necessarily move on with the first hot guy to buy me a drink, but a night of dancing and flirting would go a long way to help.

His eyes flashed as he picked up on my flirting and gave me a cocky smirk. "Noah. My name is Noah, and yours?" He held out his hand to me and I took it, letting him lead me to the dance floor.

"Juniper, or just June."

The song was a slow one, a country song that I wasn't quite familiar with, but I allowed him to pull me in close, my nose wrinkling at the strong whiff of his cologne that I got. It smelled a little like the aftershave my dad had used. Not that it was a terrible smell, just that it didn't lend to me wanting to replace the image and scent of Cade in my life.

His hands drifted down over my waist, and I tried my best not to flinch when I felt a sweaty palm make contact with my exposed skin. I instantly regretted choosing the yellow mid-drift shirt I was wearing. The song played on as we swayed to the music, completely off beat. Each second that passed, all I could do was smell his cologne and feel the stickiness of his hands gliding over my skin. What had I been thinking? This had been a horrible idea. I pulled back to excuse myself and thank him for the dance, when suddenly Noah's eyes went wide, and he was jerked back as if by some invisible force.

No, not an invisible force at all.

Cade.

## 18

### CADE

I'd watched her from my dark corner of the bar, since the moment she'd stepped foot inside. She had no clue I was there, and I was happy to keep it that way. For the past couple of days I'd kept my distance from her, but never too far. I'd just tracked her movements, noted when she left for work and came home, and anyone that she spoke to.

Dean hadn't been back to the shop since the day he'd gotten into the fight, and part of me was grateful. I wasn't sure if I would be able to hide what I was doing from him for long, and I didn't like the idea of using him for information on his sister. Whatever happened between me and Juniper, I hoped that Dean would be kept out of it. The boy had suffered enough loss, already.

A few times, I saw her gaze sweep over the spot where I was hiding in the shadows, as if she was searching for something. But she never saw me. I wondered briefly what I'd do if she did. Would she approach me? Would I approach her? Could we talk and act like normal people around each other for more than five-seconds without wanting to fuck or fight?

I swallowed hard as she tipped her head back and laughed at something one of her friends had said. The light from the neon sign their booth was sitting under, cast her skin in a pink and purple glow, giving her an ethereal look. I sucked in a breath when I saw her slide out of her seat and stretch her arms up in the air, exposing more of her stomach in the yellow mid-drift shirt she was wearing, instantly making me want to gouge the eyes out of every man in there, who watched her like I did. Instead, I ordered a whiskey on the rocks and settled further into my seat as she moved away to the dance floor with her friends. Drinking wasn't something I normally did, given what I saw with my father; but on a night like tonight, I needed to take the edge off.

My eyes narrowed when she came back from the dance floor, panting and laughing with her girlfriends, when a guy approached their table. I snorted when I saw who it was and sipped my drink, positive that Juniper would turn him down. But then to my rising anger, she gave him a slow, sensual once over, allowing him to lead her to the dance floor. Tightening the fingers on my glass, I watched as his hands grabbed her hips, pulling her closer to him. Her arms snaked up around his shoulders as they swayed together, to the sad country ballad that was playing. His hands slid from her hips, to the bare skin of her waist and she pulled back, staring up at him.

The next thing I knew, I had Noah by the throat and was snarling into his face. I didn't even remember getting up from my seat and crossing the bar.

"Get the fuck away from her."

"Cade!" Juniper's voice snapped at me, as she gaped at me in shock, but I didn't look at her. I only had eyes for the shithead who was squirming in front of me, his eyes wide with fear.

"Dude! What's your problem? We were just dancing." He sputtered the words while gasping for air, as I squeezed his windpipe. With his face turning purple under my grip, his fake bravado would have made me smile if it wasn't for the fact that all I could see were his hands on Juniper's body. Her face staring up at his, lips parted as if they— I shut down the thought. If I went there, I might kill him. The intensity of that emotion was sobering.

"Oh yeah? And does your wife know you were 'just dancing' Noah? Or did you conveniently forget to tell her you were coming home late tonight?"

"What? You're *married!?*" Juniper shrieked and I released Noah from my grip, not caring that he stumbled back. People were beginning to turn and stare.

Noah's face turned red. "Fuck you Cade. You don't know what you're talking about."

Before I could respond, Juniper slipped between us. "No, fuck *you*, Noah. Clearly he knows enough to know that you are a married man, out here buying drinks for girls behind his wife's back. How about you go home and work that out before you start trying to shoot your shot." She snarled at him. "Oh, and by the way, you smell like an old man. Maybe change the cologne and your wife will like you enough to give you another chance, even though she deserves way better."

And then, she was storming off through the gathered crowd leaving both me and Noah staring after her. I shoved past him, not able to resist giving him one last push, and followed her, catching up to her as she reached the edge of the dance floor. I grabbed her arm stopping her and she whirled on me, her eyes furious and full of something I didn't expect to see, tears.

I didn't know what made me say it, but the worlds tumbled before I could stop them. "Dance with me."

"What?" The statement must have shocked her just as much as it did me. But now that I'd said it, I knew that's exactly what I wanted. Her in my arms, my hands on her skin, my body moving with hers and erasing every second of that shithead who thought he could ever have a chance with her, from her mind. I stepped in closer just as the next song started and the familiar chords to Mazzy Star's, "Fade Into You" began to play. Fitting. "Dance with me, pretty girl." My hand cupped her chin as I traced my thumb along her plump bottom lip and smirked. "Unless you're scared?"

Her eyes flashed with wariness but she didn't back away. "I'm not scared of you, Cade Black."

I pulled her to me, the other couples dancing around us, fading into the background. Her body fit to mine like it was made to move there. My hands traced the skin along her spine, and I heard her suck in her breath in a soft gasp. She smelled faintly of citrus and lavender. Bitter and sweet all at the same time. Leaning down so that my lips were just pressed to the tender flesh of her ear, I whispered, "Maybe you should be."

She shivered against me and not from the cold. I could see her flesh pebble, nipples hardening beneath the thin shirt she wore. *Fuck*. She wasn't wearing a bra. I wanted to find Noah, rip his cock off and feed it to him.

"Why Cade? Why should I be scared?" She pulled her head away, forcing me to look down at her, as the music swelled around us. Her lips were parted, blue eyes glistening as they pierced through me. "Because you're angry with me? Because I betrayed you and now you hate me for it?" She shook her head. "I'm not scared of your rage or your anger, Cade. I'm not scared of what revenge you'll take out on me. I deserve it." Her hand reached up, fingers tracing the edge of my scar with a featherlight, almost reverent touch. A scar I'd received because I was thrown into a prison I should have never been in. "The only thing I'm scared of, is what the price of your revenge will do to my heart."

I kissed her. I couldn't help it. It was the only thing that could drown out the thundering sound of blood, rushing in my ears as her words drove knives into my soul. She knew she'd betrayed me. She didn't deny it, didn't back away from it. Didn't apologize for it either. I'd wanted her confession to come with her on her knees before me, begging for forgiveness. But this was different, this was a quiet acknowledgement of the pain she'd caused, and the understanding that she would need to pay the price for it.

It wasn't a gentle kiss. I poured every ounce of anger, rage, and hurt that I felt into it. Her lips parted under mine, our tongues sliding together, the dark desire that had been churning under the surface roaring to life. Desire that I'd kept under careful lock and key all these years, until the day I'd driven back into city and saw her standing on the sidewalk. I understood then. There wasn't a distraction, a place, an escape that could ease the ache in my soul, that Juniper had left behind. It was her. Only her.

I pulled away, staring down into those startling, blue eyes that were glazed over with lust, lips parted and swollen from my kiss.

"Come with me." Her eyes widened at my

demand and I thought for a moment she'd refuse. "I need to show you something."

A small frown creased her brow, but she nodded and I took her hand, leading her away from the dance floor and toward the exit. She paused for a brief second to grab her jacket and purse from her friends, who cast worried and suspicious glances at me. Then we walked out the door into the crisp, Colorado night air.

The feel of her hands on my stomach, her body pressed against my back, the way she tightened her grip and slid in close to me as we took sharp turns, brought back memories. Memories that my anger had kept pushed away in a dark corner of my heart.

We pulled up to B's Custom Creations and I parked the bike. She slid off behind me, removing the extra helmet I'd given her, placing it on the seat.

"You wanted to show me your shop?" She arched one blonde brow, but her tone was curious.

I didn't say anything, just walked to the door and hit the code that would disable the alarm, before opening the door. She followed behind me silently as I made my way back to the mechanic's bay door.

I opened the door and reached for the light switch panel next to it, flicking on all the lights on, illuminating the entire bay. Her gasp of surprise almost made me smile. Rows upon rows of bays were lit up. Bikes of all kinds and in all stages of customization were sitting in them. There were twenty in total, ten on one side and ten on the other. At the far end of the shop, was a paint booth for the custom paint jobs, beyond that was a private parts warehouse.

Juniper moved past me, walking past each bike, taking in the details, the size and the enormity of the entire operation. Finally, she stopped and looked back at me. "Which one is yours?"

I smirked. "Technically they're all mine."

She rolled her eyes. "Yeah, yeah. You're the owner. I know that now." She gestured towards the bays. "Fine, I'll figure it out myself."

I wondered if she would. All the tool boxes and items were identical with the shop's logo emblazoned on them. But each mechanic had their own way of setting up their bay and putting their stamp on it. No two were alike. I watched as she walked up and down the center of the shop, examining each bay carefully. Then she stopped in front of one at the end and I sucked in a breath.

She turned with a grin and pointed. "This one is yours."

I moved to stand in front of her. "How can you be sure? They all look a lot alike."

Looking up at me, her lips curled into a smirk. "Because it's the cleanest."

I chuckled, the sound surprising me. It must have surprised her too because her eyes danced with delight as she moved to where the Honda cafe racer was assembled, waiting for its turn in the paint bay.

"You did it." She traced her hand along my black tool box, her fingers grazing over the logo. "Even after my dad ruined everything, you made your dreams come true." Her voice was soft with emotion, and when she looked at me, her gaze was filled with pride. My chest tightened as feelings I didn't understand or want to think about, bubbled up.

"No thanks to you."

Pain replaced the look of pride in her eyes and hardened my heart. She nodded. "Yeah, no thanks to me." She raised her chin a notch and stepped in closer, her bright, floral scent flooding my senses. "Is that why you brought me here? To remind me of what I fucked up? Because I promise you Cade Black, there hasn't been a day that's gone by for the past five years where I haven't thought about it, and regretted every single second of that night."

I shook my head. Yes, it had been partly why I'd

brought her here. I'd wanted to see how she'd react. Would she seek to ruin me again? I grabbed the back of her head, pulling it back as I wound her thick hair in my hands. Crushing her to me, her eyes went wide in surprise. "No, pretty girl, I brought you here to do this."

And then for the second time that night, I kissed her.

## 19

### JUNIPER

*I*'d been so sure he'd brought me here to tell me how much he hated me, and to rub his success in my face after what my family had done to his family. But then, his hands were in my hair, his lips moving over mine and I was lost to the sensation of being totally and completely consumed by him. For a brief moment, I thought I should tell him to stop. That I should step away and give ourselves space. There was too much between us. Too many secrets. Too many lies. Too much time.

But then it was like the last chink to the armor I'd tried to place around my heart collapsed, and none of it mattered anymore. All I could hear was his name, like a drum beat in my ears. *Cade. Cade. Cade.*

He growled against my lips when my arms came

up to wrap around his shoulders, pressing myself harder against him.

"Tell me you don't have a fiancé anymore. Tell me you're not married."

I shook my head. "No Cade, there's no fiancé or husband, there never was."

His teeth nipped at my lips, "Another lie." But before I could question him, he was stealing my breath away with another kiss, and his hands were at the button of my jeans, tugging them down. I stopped him just long enough to step out of my shoes, and then the next thing I knew, he was placing me on the seat of the cafe racer in his bay. He grabbed my hips, scooting me to the edge and then hooked his thumbs under the lace edge of my panties. When he'd pulled them off and tossed them to the side, he stood back, looking down on me.

"Spread your legs."

He wasn't asking. It was a demand. My breath hitched, and his eyes never looked away from mine as I slowly spread my legs apart, exposing everything to him. His eyes flicked down, darkening, and didn't look away.

"Wider."

When I hesitated, he leaned down, dragging his lips up the side of my neck, and placed both of his hands on my knees, pushing my legs further apart. "I spent two years in prison, thinking about nothing but the revenge I would get when I got out. And when I wasn't thinking about revenge, I was thinking about this moment right here. If you want to pay the price for betraying me, this is it. Now spread your legs for me, pretty girl. Show me that pretty little pussy."

I gasped, his words, the dirtiness of them and the way he growled against my skin, sent moisture pooling right to my very core. Right to the very spot his eyes locked onto, when he felt my legs fall open at his demand. "Prison?" I breathed the question.

He ignored me as he removed his leather jacket and shirt. My mouth went dry at the sight of him, naked from the waist up. The tattoos I'd peeked under his shirt sleeves, continued across his chest.

They were my designs.

The designs I'd drawn for him all those years ago. Skulls that peeked out from beneath the petals of wildflowers, and the mountains of our home lined the hard planes of his chest in deep, vivid colors of blue, purple and gray. Then, he knelt before me, his large hands tracing my thighs, breathing in my scent before glancing up at me. The scar on his face, and the dark glint in his eyes made him look absolutely wicked. Like he was a beast about to devour his prey. Me.

"I waited. I thought you'd come for me and I waited." His hot breath fanned my sensitive flesh and I squirmed, but his hands kept me still. "It wasn't until the judge handed down my sentence, that I finally accepted that you weren't coming. That you were truly gone." His tongue flicked out, tasting me and I panted, trying to understand what he was telling me, but was wholly distracted by the sight and feel of him between my legs.

"I don't understand. I didn't know anything had happened." Hazel eyes narrowed at my words, and his fingers dug into my hips, gripping me tighter.

"Maybe you did. Maybe you didn't. But I spent the next seven hundred and thirty-five days remembering how you tasted on my tongue, then another three years after that, trying to forget." His lips trailed kisses on the inside of my thigh. "And now I'm going to live out every fantasy I ever had while I was rotting in the cell that your father put me in. That's my revenge. That's my price."

And then his tongue and lips were devouring me, as if I were his last meal. His hands moved under my ass, lifting and pulling me towards him as he sucked and nibbled on my clit, sending spikes of pleasure through me.

When I cried out, he pulled back, lips glistening with my arousal, and gave me a feral grin. He withdrew a hand from under me to run his fingers through my wetness, teasing my opening. "Look how messy you are, pretty girl. Tell me, how often did you think about what we did that day in the barn?"

My head fell back when he thrust his fingers into me, curling them to hit that sweet spot before pulling them out again. "Almost every damn day."

"Hmm..." He pushed them back in again, slowly filling me, and I gasped when I felt his other hand slip down to tease another sensitive area. "That's not good enough. I wanted you thinking about it every minute, every second of every day. I wanted it haunting you. Because that's exactly what it did to me." And then his fingers plunged into my openings the same time that his tongue sucked and teased my clit. I bucked, the sensations overwhelming me until I felt like I was coming apart at the seams.

He pulled away and stood back up, while I was left panting and breathless on the bike.

"On your knees." He growled out the command, and I raised my head enough to see him slide the zipper to his jeans down as he began to peel them over his hips. His cock sprang free, and I slid from the bike to the floor, kneeling on his leather jacket. He looked down at me, the gold flashing in his eyes. "I thought about this too. I wanted you just like this, saying you're sorry. Begging me to forgive you."

I watched as his hand stroked the thick length, coming closer to me. "And did you?' My eyes flicked back up to his, licking my lips. "Did you forgive me?"

A cruel smile curved the corner of his lips. "No." Then his cock was sliding past my lips, my tongue swirling around the head and thick shaft, as he forced it further and further down my throat. He groaned, a guttural sound. "Fuck, it's better than I imagined." His hands gripped my hair as he pulled me to him, using my mouth and throat as if he was caught up in the fantasy again. He looked down at me, watching as he slid his cock past my lips until it hit the back of my throat, then he'd pull back out, only to slam back in again.

Then, just when I thought I wouldn't be able to catch my breath, I was pulled up, my shirt ripped off over my head before I was flipped over. He placed my hands on the handlebars of the bike and spread my legs over the seat, so that I was straddling it with my bare feet on the cold, concrete floor. My nipples brushed against the cold metal of the cafe racer's gas tank, and I hissed.

I heard the rip of a condom and felt him settle behind me. His fingers wound into my hair as he pulled my head back, harshly so that my spine arched.

His lips grazed my ear, his voice growling into it. "Tell me you want this, pretty girl. Tell me you need this as much as I do."

"I do. Fuck, Cade, I do. I needed it then and I need it now."

He chuckled darkly and I felt his cock pressing against my opening."Good girl. Hold on, tight."

And then he was filling me. Driving into me with hard, firm strokes until I was gripping the handlebars and hanging on for dear life. He set the rhythm, his hips slamming into me, cock gliding through my pussy, over the spot deep inside until I was a shaking mess. His hands let go of my hair and settled on my hips, pulling me back against him until I took over the pace, needing more. I worked my hips back against him, impaling myself on his thick heat. I felt his hand glide from my hips, over my ass, then the sharp sting of his palm against my cheek.

"That's it baby, fuck yourself on my cock."

His words had me gushing, giving me something

I didn't know I needed. I tipped my head back, screaming as the orgasm ripped through me.

He took over then, pounding into me with a punishing pace, and all I could do was hold on for dear life, as another orgasm began to build.

Bending over me, he drove his hips down, kneading my breasts with his hands. The angle of his thrusts put friction on my clit against the leather seat of the motorcycle, and I sobbed with need. Not since the day in the barn had I been filled like this, tormented like this, or left such a blubbering mess that all I could utter over and over again was, "Please, Cade, please."

He sat back, but kept me pressed against the seat with a hand on my back. "That's it, Juniper. Come for me again. Come on my cock, pretty girl."

Every muscle and nerve ending in my body tensed as the orgasm tore through me once more. I cried out in protest when he withdrew, and gathered me in his arms. The next thing I knew, he was stalking toward his office.

"Where are we going?"

Without ceremony I was dumped on his desk, scattering papers and pens everywhere before he spread my legs, lining himself up with my opening. "I have a new fantasy now. One I've been thinking about ever since you walked through that door." And then he was kissing me at the same time that he filled me, once more. The kiss was brutal, just as brutal as his hips driving into mine. There was a desperation to it, a need. A need that matched my own. My legs locked around his waist as I pulled him into me. My hands tangling in his hair. His lips left mine and he pulled back, grabbing my wrists with one hand and pinning them to the desk above my head.

I couldn't move. All I could do was take. And I did, over and over again until once more, I was begging and pleading with him to give me what I so desperately needed. He pulled back, sliding his hand between our sweat-slick bodies, finding that sweet nub of nerves, but he didn't stroke it, didn't tease it. Instead, he kept his fingers just out of reach until I sobbed. "I need it, Cade, please!"

"Not until you say it, pretty girl." He slammed into me, the tips of his fingers just grazing my clit, but it wasn't enough. My nails dug into his hips. I needed more. "Fucking say it, Juniper!" He snarled.

"I'm sorry!" I tipped my head back and screamed. "I'm so fucking sorry I lied."

Something snapped in him, and he grabbed my throat with his other hand as his hips hammered into me. At the same time, the fingers he'd kept just out of reach pinched my clit, sending a shockwave of pain and pleasure through me. I came, screaming my release until my throat felt raw and the edges of my vision went black.

He collapsed on me, sweaty and gasping for breath, his body heavy on mine. But I didn't notice, didn't care, because every muscle and limb was still spasming from the aftershocks of the orgasms he'd given me. I barely registered as he carefully disentangled himself from me, pulling the condom from him and throwing it in a nearby waste bin. I could only sigh when he gathered me in his arms, walking me over to the couch where he collapsed with me on his chest.

I grumbled slightly, and started to raise my head up when I felt him pull a scratchy blanket from the back of the couch over our bodies, tucking it around us. But all he did was place a soft, almost featherlight kiss on my forehead. "Sleep, pretty girl." He commanded. And so I did.

## 20

### CADE

*I* wasn't sure how long I had dozed, but I woke to her soft snoring on my chest, her mouth parted just slightly as she dreamed. Conflicting emotions twisted my gut and knowing I wouldn't be able to go back to sleep, I gently tucked the blanket around her and slipped free. I made my way back to my bay area where I gathered up our clothes, wiped away the mess she'd left on the leather seat of my client's cafe racer, and made a mental note to offer him whatever price he wanted for it. He wasn't getting it back.

I pulled my jeans back on, then picked up my jacket, pulling my phone free to see I had several missed calls. Hitting the "redial" button, he picked up on the first ring.

"About fucking time. Have a good night reconnecting?"

My grip on my phone tightened. "How the fuck did you know what I was doing, Kage?"

His dark laughter filled my ears. "Did you really think I'd leave you all on your own? I have my eyes and ears."

"So you're watching the watcher." Fucking asshole. I knew it wouldn't be as cut and dry with him as he'd said it would be.

"Always, Cade. Always. But it's not what you think. I'm protecting my investments and looking out for a friend, that's all."

I frowned. "Well, if you're calling to see if I've found out anything, you're out of luck. I've got nothing that we don't already know."

"You'll have to do better than that. You don't have much time." I heard the *clink* of ice in a glass on the other end of the line, and checked the time on my watch, 3:00am.

"You're up late, and you've been stalking me like a jealous ex-girlfriend. You better start talking or the deal's off. I'll sell every damn thing I own to pay you back, and then you can go chasing after Edmund Wild's ghost on your own." I growled into the phone. The secrecy and bullshit games Kage liked to play were starting to get on my nerves. And after tonight with Juniper, I didn't know that I had the heart or the desire to betray her anymore. Her confession, her adamant denial of knowing that I'd been thrown into prison, or why, and the cry of her apology as I'd wrung out every last bit of an orgasm from her body, had left me shaken to the core. How much had been Juniper's fault, and how much had been the schemes of her father? More than that, how much had been my own twisted skew of the situation because I was so biased toward her family?

Kage's voice was ice-cold as it slithered through my ear. "And who would buy it? Who would be willing to take on your debt, knowing I was the one who held your reins? I own you, Cade Black and I've been a very lenient man until now. Do not force my hand."

My jaw clenched, "Don't do this, Kage. You don't want to make us enemies. We've been friends for too long. Don't forget who your man was on the inside when I was in the pen. I know where the bodies are buried, Kage, because I helped fucking bury them. But I'll uncover every single one if it means Juniper is kept safe." I gritted through my teeth. And I meant it. Even if it meant landing right back in the place that I'd spent every waking hour, wishing I was away from. "You need to start telling me the truth. What do you want with her?"

The other end of the line was deadly quiet for several heartbeats, and for a moment, I thought he'd hung up on me. But then his voice came in on the other end once more. "You're right." He sighed, and for the first time since I'd known him, I thought I could hear a tinge of stress and worry in his voice. "I don't want us to be enemies. I have very few friends and people I trust. You are one of them."

It wasn't an apology, but it would do, and some of the tension I held, eased. I didn't want to go to war with Kage, and I certainly didn't want to work for him, but he was a friend, and I would help him however I could. "Then let me help you. Tell me what's really going on."

He cleared his throat. "This is a story that's too long to tell you over the phone, or at three o'clock in the morning. But I'll say this, and whatever you do, you can't tell Juniper. Her life is in danger and believe it or not, I'm trying to protect her."

Fear like a vice grip, squeezed my pounding heart in my chest. "What do you mean she's in danger? How the fuck do you know any of this?"

"Because there are forces at play here that are bigger than a family name, bigger than a city, bigger than you and me. And the key to all of it, is sleeping naked on the couch in your office, at this very moment. You need to protect her, even if it's from herself."

"How the fuck do you know she's naked—" I cut myself off, it didn't matter. "Never mind. Who is after her? What forces are you talking about?"

"Enemies you wouldn't even know of, yet. But for right now? The biggest threat to your little wildflower is the man she calls her father, Edmund Wild."

I paced up and down the bay, the urge to run into the office and check on her, nearly overwhelming me, but I didn't want to wake her up. "Her father is dead." I growled into the phone.

"Her father is dead, that's true. Edmund Wild is not."

I froze. His words hitting me like a freight train.

"Edmund Wild is not her father?"

"No, he's not." Kage replied.

"If he's not her father, then who is?"

He sighed, sounding tired. "I wish I could tell you more. But for right now, I can't. Just know that so long as Edmund is alive, Juniper is in danger. He needs her, and he will stop at nothing to get her back into his clutches again. I fucked up when I had her here, thinking he wouldn't dare try and come after her while she was with me. I didn't count on other people coming into play, or that he'd get so desperate. Just trust me when I say that he's coming for her, and she needs your protection."

Rage, colder and darker than anything I'd ever felt before, descended on me. "How long have you known?"

"Not as long as you think. When she came to me at Club Diablo it was pure coincidence. I had no idea who she was then, but I did some digging, and when I learned she was Edmund Wild's daughter I thought I'd have some leverage on him, so I let her stay. It wasn't until later that I found out he wasn't her real dad at all."

Some of the suspicion eased, but the rage remained. "Do you know where he is now?"

"No, I have some leads and I'm working on trying to find him, but he's as slippery as they come. Which is why I need you to keep your eye on her and watch her close. I have no doubt that he's biding his time, waiting for whatever pieces in this game that he's playing, to fall into place. But until I know more, I don't want her alarmed. She'll just run and then he'll have her right where he wants her."

I ran my fingers through my hair in frustration. There was so much that Kage wasn't telling me, I could feel it. "This has to do with her family history doesn't it? The pact the families made when they came to Wild generations ago?"

"Yes." He said, and I could hear him adding more ice to his glass. "I want to tell you, Cade, but I don't have all the information yet. Please just trust me. There's a reason she's back in Wild. There's a reason that cursed place won't let her go."

My jaw clenched in frustration. Juniper, *my* Juniper, was in danger from a man that wasn't even her dad. A man that had bullied and manipulated her for years. I seethed. "When you find him, he's mine. The kill is mine."

He chuckled darkly once more. "Ah, there's the ruthless Black coming out to play. Maybe you aren't the choir boy you've been trying to pretend to be all these years? Maybe you'll decide you want to get back on the train ride to Hell after all."

"Don't push it, Kage." I bit out.

I could feel his sinister grin through the phone. "Fine. The kill is yours. Protect her and trust no one." Then he hung up, and I was left staring at the phone as red hazed over my vision.

In prison, it had been "fend for yourself or die". The gang wars from the outside often bled into the steel and concrete walls of the penitentiary. At the time, Kage had just risen to his rank as President of the Sons of Diablo, but it had not been without bloodshed. He'd come to me, still cementing his place in the organization, and we'd made a deal. He knew I'd never have spilled my father's secrets, and the secrets of the club, and we both had agreed that the organization needed to change. What happened to my dad should never happen again. It was time for the old ways of doing things to go away, to make way for a new, more modern era of doing business. But to do that, Kage needed to weed-out the garden and make room for new growth. And I was his tool.

I spent the next two years behind bars, being both his spy, and his death dealer. My hands were bloody with the sentences I handed down on those who opposed him. The skulls that danced up my arms, half-hidden in shadows of smoke and flames, were the testament to my kills. I wasn't proud of it. But I had done it to survive, and to protect my father. After two years, we'd cut a bloody path, me from the inside, Kage from the outside, through anyone who'd opposed him and the changes he wanted to make. When it was done, he'd gotten me my freedom, having uncovered the real arsonist behind the Fuller barn fire, and I was released. But when he'd offered me a place at his side, I'd refused.

No matter what modern era he brought the Sons of Diablo into, it was a life that I didn't want to be a part of any longer. We'd parted ways, with him loaning me the money I needed to start my business because I refused to take it as a gift. I would build it the right way, the hard way, and finally have a name I could be proud of.

I gripped the phone so tight the screen shattered in my hands. But if it meant protecting Juniper, if it meant keeping her safe and getting revenge on the sick bastard who was threatening her? I would hop back on that dark train again in a heartbeat. Only I wouldn't ride it to Hell. No, I'd bring all of Hell back with me.

## 21

### JUNIPER

I awoke to the scent of leather, and the alluring aroma of fresh coffee. Blinking sleep out of my eyes, I sat up and realized I'd been wrapped in Cade's leather jacket, my legs covered with the blanket from last night, and I was still on the couch in his office.

"Morning, sunshine." His voice grumbled at me, and I looked up to see him standing in the office doorway, a styrofoam cup of coffee in his hand, a lazy smile on his lips. His hair was down, and I realized it was much longer and thicker than I had thought, now that it was out of the bun. It brushed the top of his shoulders and my fingers itched to play with it.

I knew without glancing down that I was still

naked, and hugged his jacket to my chest. As if sensing my panic, he held out the coffee to me, "Don't worry. Shop's closed, we don't open on Sundays unless we need to."

"Well, that's good. I didn't exactly feel like doing the walk of shame past your receptionist. Something tells me she wouldn't have been too happy about it." I relaxed and took the cup from him, eyeing it suspiciously. "Did you—" but he cut me off.

"French vanilla creamer and two sugars. I remembered." He gave me a wink and suddenly I was too hot under his jacket.

"Oh." I took a sip of my coffee to distract myself from the thoughts and emotions that were fluttering around in my head. Something about him was different this morning. He seemed softer, less on-edge. The mind-blowing sex may have had something to do with it, but I couldn't be sure.

I sat up further. "Cade listen, we should probably talk about last night." The jacket slid down my chest before I could grab it, and his eyes darkened immediately as they landed on my exposed breasts. I scrambled to pull it back up over me. "And I should probably get some clothes on before we have that conversation."

"I don't know. I think I might prefer the conversation as-is." His smirk was feral, but he walked to his desk and picked up a pile of clothing before handing it to me. They were my things, washed and folded neatly, right down to my panties. I blinked in surprise. "You washed my clothes?"

He shrugged nonchalantly. "We have a washer and dryer here for anyone to use. There's a shower too if you want to clean up first."

"Thank you." I said softly, as I wrapped the blanket around me and stood up. The change in his attitude had me feeling off-balance. My heart was doing flips in my chest, while my mind was desperately trying to pump the brakes before I jumped off the ledge of conclusions. Multiple orgasms and the best sex of my life, did not automatically mean that things were ok between us.

Suddenly, I felt a finger under my chin, forcing my eyes up to look into his. "If you don't stop frowning like that I'm going to think that I didn't do a good enough job making you scream as you came last night, and that I'll need to rectify that immediately."

I gasped, licking my lips as every part of me turned to liquid heat. "No, that's not it at all."

His lips brushed against mine. A soft, tender kiss that had me leaning towards him for more, before he pulled away with a smirk. "Good. Go shower, pretty girl. We'll finish this later."

I hurried out of the office and to the shop where he'd directed me to go. It was a basic shower stall, but I'd found shampoo and everything there I'd need to freshen up. When I was done and dressed, I used a towel to dry my hair the best I could before finger-combing it and pulling it back into a messy braid.

Walking back into the main mechanics bay, I found Cade waiting for me, a helmet in hand. I took it from him. "I should probably be getting home." He nodded and put his helmet on before waiting for me to climb on the bike behind him. I tried not to let my disappointment show as I clipped-on my own helmet, while settling into my seat. I barely had time to grab onto his waist before he roared out of the mechanics bay, and onto the road that would lead us to the mountain highways.

Anxiety roiled in my stomach as I replayed the events of last night. The confession about his time in prison. The implied accusation that I'd been responsible for it, and once again questioning whether or not I had a fiancé. Something wasn't adding up. There was something important that I was missing, and I tried to recall everything Cade had said or done since the night at the barn. But I couldn't put the pieces together. I had more questions than answers at this point. As my mind drifted, I failed to notice where we were going until he'd turned down a gravel road that looked hauntingly familiar.

The bike came to a stop at what looked like the burned-down ruins of a building. A barn. I gasped as I removed my helmet and slid off the seat behind him. It was our barn.

"What happened?"

He came up behind me and his face was an unreadable mask. No emotions showing as he observed me. "Arson. It was set on fire with Jim Fuller inside."

My jaw dropped in shock. "Oh my God, was he ok? When did this happen?"

"He survived, barely." He cocked his head slightly, gaze piercing through me. "The night you left."

Pieces started to click into place.

"Oh God. They thought you did it." My hand covered my mouth as I realized what he was saying. "And I was gone. I couldn't be your alibi."

He nodded slowly and then moved away from me to stand at the edge of what had once been the great barn doors. "When you left, I drove for hours trying to find you. I wanted to apologize for what happened," he cleared his throat. "No, that's not true. I didn't regret what happened, just the *how*."

I didn't say anything and let him continue on. There was no need to tell him that I only regretted the same thing. The *how*, not the *what*.

"Sheriff Joley found me about an hour away from the city. I don't even remember how I got there." He snorted and shook his head. "I should have found it suspicious that he seemed to know exactly where I was, and found me so quickly after the fire was put out, and Jim was pulled from the ashes." He turned back to me, and my heart flinched at the pain I saw there.

"I thought you'd abandoned me, Juniper. I thought you were angry with me for what had happened and were content to just let me rot in prison for the rest of my life. And I thought that because that's what I felt like I deserved."

"Cade, no!" I moved toward him, hands coming up to cup his face so that he was forced to look down at me. "I had no idea any of this happened. I never went home. I'd never had any intention of going back home that night either."

He nodded, "I know that now, June. But I didn't then. When you couldn't be found to collaborate my story they called your dad. And he said you'd never been with me that night, that you had left to go and stay with your fiancé's family for awhile, to prepare for your wedding."

I gasped, in shock. "There was never a fiancé, Cade. At least, not one I agreed to."

His arms came to wrap around me and I buried my face in his jacket, breathing in the scent of leather and open road that was uniquely him. He rested his chin on the top of my head. "I'm sorry Juniper. I don't know what else to say, but I'm sorry. I should have listened to you, believed you. I see now that you couldn't have betrayed me. Your dad betrayed us both."

I flinched at his words and pulled away. "Cade you have no reason to apologize. At least not for that."

He looked down at me, a small frown on his face. "What do you mean?"

I sighed and moved away from him as I turned to observe the ruins of the barn. "I did tell my father about your dad's loan." Tears began to form, and swallowed them back. "And I know that, you know that, but you don't know why."

"So why then?" His voice was a low grumble behind me, but then I felt his arms slip around my waist. "Why did you lie, pretty girl?"

"Because he made me choose." A sob came as the memory came back to me. A night I'd buried deep down.

*My brother asleep on the couch in my father's study. My father sitting in front of the fireplace, his face half-hidden in the shadows.*

*"Choose, Juniper. Your duty, or your brother." The flames from the fireplace glinted off the metal of his gun. My heart racing as I looked between the sleeping face of my brother, and the unfeeling mask my father wore. He didn't care that at any minute, Dean could wake up and see him like this. That he would see the monster our father really was.*

*"You can't make me do this." I'd whispered the words as tears had flowed down my face.*

*He smiled, but there was nothing warm or soft about it. "You're right. I can't force you, unfortunately, to walk the path before you. I can only encourage you by whatever means necessary." He shifted the barrel of his gun on his knee just slightly so that it was pointed at Dean. My heart froze. He wouldn't.*

*"Papa, please." My voice cracked with emotion. "Don't do this."*

*He leaned forward, smile curling at the corners of his lips, but there was nothing warm or fatherly about it. "Sweet girl, you leave me no choice. You resist me at every turn. What else am I to do but apply a little,"* His finger twitched slightly on the trigger and I fell to my knees in fear, *"...pressure."*

"That night I came to you in the barn. I was going to confess. I was going to tell you everything." I hugged myself around my stomach. "But then I realized it was all a sick game my father was playing. He made me choose between you and my brother, when he already knew. He already had the information he needed to destroy your father. I realized it as soon as you showed me the letter from the bank, and told me he'd been by the store. It was all part of his plan."

My shoulders slumped. "But I still told him. I still set out to help him and I never told you about it. I never let you know that he was trying to ruin any chance you had of turning your life around." Silent tears fell.

He was silent for a moment, then he turned me around so that I was facing him. And when I refused to look up, he gripped my jaw in his hands and forced my eyes on him.

"Juniper we were young and foolish. I knew you were a trap from the moment you'd walked up to me at the hardware store and asked me for help. I wasn't dumb, I just didn't care. You were worth the risk." His thumb grazed over the bottom of my lip. "The only thing I regret is letting your father's words get into my head. I knew I shouldn't have believed him. I knew I should have just asked you to explain, and given you a chance. But I let our family's history and my hatred of your dad, blind me. I'm so sorry." And then he was kissing me.

22

CADE

I kissed her, and this time there was no anger or rage behind it. It was a kiss that begged her to forgive me for not believing her. For thinking that she was anything at all like her father. Her mouth parted under mine and I became instantly hard. The memories from last night replaying in my head. We were out in the open, with the morning air still chilled against our skin, but damn if I didn't want to take her again, right there. Right in the ruined ashes of the barn where she'd given herself to me completely the first time. The memory made me flinch. That's not how I'd wanted to do it. She deserved more.

Her fingers worked their way under my jacket

and found the edges of my t-shirt, skimming along my ribs and dipping down to the waistband of my jeans, as if she was thinking the same thing. I pulled back, "Let me take you home, to a real bed," her stomach growled, "...and after, I'll cook you breakfast."

There was a mischievous twinkle in her eye as her fingers played with the button to my jeans, and then before I could protest, she'd undid them and slipped her hand inside, palming my cock. "Is that what you really want to do, Cade? Are you the gentlemen ready to cater to my every need?" She stroked my length and I bit back a groan. "Or is the *real* Cade the one who fucked me last night? The one who made me beg and scream. What does *that* Cade want to do right now?"

Something dark sparked inside of me. Part of me had been afraid that how I'd been with her in my shop, had been too much, too rough, too wild. But here she was, challenging me to do it again. Almost as if she knew that I'd always held back that side of me when I was with her.

I leaned down, gripping her chin my hand again, a little tighter. "Be careful what you wish for, pretty girl." She licked her lips, her blue eyes dark with desire.

"You're all I ever wished for, Cade Black."

I snarled, and jerked her hand out of my pants at the protest of my aching cock. "Get on the bike, Juniper. You want me to fuck you? Fine. But I'll do it on my terms." Her throaty laugh as I stalked away adjusting myself as I went, made me want to turn around, bend her over my knee and spank her smart ass until it was red. The image of her bare cheeks, tinged pink with my handprint, made me nearly explode in my pants. But I refused to take her there in the dirt like before. She might be ok with it, but I was not. Not yet at least.

I slammed my helmet over my head as if it could somehow block out all the dirty thoughts running through my head, and then I felt her hands slip around my waist and I kicked the bike into gear, roaring onto the road that would lead to her home.

Juniper's confession had stunned me. I knew her dad was a real asshole, but I'd never imagined that he'd force Juniper to make a choice like that. Blacks and Wilds had never been on good terms. And while both our families frequently found themselves on the opposite sides of the law, the Wilds always seemed to walk away without a scratch, while my family had earned their reputation as drunks and hard-asses. You could say that one was blue collar and one was white collar, and the two did not cross the street to greet each other.

Yet, something about the situation seemed off. Blackmailing her into betraying me and then dropping the hints about her arranged marriage. All of it suddenly took on a different look, now that I knew Edmund Wild wasn't her real dad. Kage's words about "other forces being in play" stirred, and I felt a sudden twinge of guilt. Juniper didn't know that Edmund wasn't her real dad. And she didn't know that he was alive either. But Kage had insisted I keep it a secret from her, and if it meant keeping her safe, I would do that and more. At least until I knew enough to tell Kage to fuck off.

Her house came into view and I slowed down to turn into the half-circle drive. I parked the bike next to her yellow Volkswagen and took my helmet off with a grin. "You still have that piece of junk?"

She let out an indignant huff. "You take that back! Penny is not junk. She's just in need of a little TLC, which I will get to, just as soon as the emporium is up on its feet."

I frowned, the Wilds had always had money. Juniper shouldn't be scraping by to fix a half-broken down rust bucket, or driving one for that matter. I made a mental note to ask Kage to check into the state of Juniper's finances.

I circled around the car, noting that she'd need new tires before winter came, and the roads became too slick for her to drive up and down the mountain passes, stopping when I got to the hood. "Are you planning on branching out with your tattoo skills into car detailing? Because," I arched one brow at her in curiosity, "...as talented of an artist as you are, I don't think this is your best work."

"What are you talking about? I've never painted my car." She came around to look at what I was pointing to on the hood, and her face instantly turned two shades whiter as she stumbled back. She looked like she'd seen a ghost. I stepped toward her, but her eyes remained glued on the hood of her car, and the image spray painted in blood-red paint there. A skull, a crown of flames circling its head.

"You didn't paint that." It wasn't a question and I wasn't going to give her a chance to explain it away. I moved myself between her and her car, blocking her view of it and forcing her to look at me. "What's going on Juniper? Why is someone painting skulls on your car?"

She stiffened, and I could see her walls slamming

into place. She was hiding something. "I don't know. I'm sure it's just kids playing pranks."

I took another step forward, anger rising. "Don't lie to me, pretty girl. You need to tell me what's going on and you need to do it now."

Her chin raised a notch, eyes flaring stubbornly. "You don't own me, Cade, I don't need to tell you anything."

So it was going to be like that. I shook my head, a slow grin parting my lips as I advanced on her. She didn't back up, not realizing the threat until it was too late and I had her by the waist and was throwing her over my shoulder. I crossed the yard and took the stairs that led up to her house two at a time, barely side-stepping a hole in her front porch. Her fists pounded against my back.

"Put me down you jackass! You don't just pick up women and throw them over your shoulder!"

"You're right. I don't pick up women and throw them over my shoulder, just you. Now, if you want to tell me what's going on, *maybe* I'll put you down."

"You will put me down right now!"

"Nope, not happening, pretty girl." I opened her front door, surprised it was unlocked, and stepped into the cool interior. "Is anyone home right now?"

"Yes, everyone is home. You should put me down

now before they see you and think I'm being kidnapped and call the sheriff." Her tone was full of fake concern.

"Great, that means no one is home and it's just you and me." I brought my hand down on her jean-clad backside and she yelped in surprise. "And that is for lying to me, again."

"You did not just spank me!" Her voice was full of indignation and I had to bite back a chuckle.

"Yes, and if you keep up the lying, there will be plenty more spankings to come." I paused in the dimly lit hall and glanced up the stairs. "Where's your bedroom?"

She huffed. "Oh like I'm going to tell you, you neanderthal. Put me down!"

I shrugged. "Ok fine suit yourself, but I didn't think you'd want your housekeeper, what's her name? Bess? To find you in the position I plan to put you in."

I heard a soft gasp as she stilled. "What position is that?"

"Naked, on your knees and taking my cock in that pretty, lying mouth of yours until you can't stand it anymore, and are begging me to fuck your pussy."

There was a slight pause and for a moment I

thought she would go back to fighting me but then I heard her breathless reply. "Down the hall, third door on the left."

I grinned, moving down the hall, thankful she couldn't see my face and growled. "That's my pretty girl. I hope you aren't lying to me again. You're already in trouble for the car, let's not add to it."

"What are you planning?" Her voice was husky with fear and lust.

"I'm planning to show you exactly how wrong you are. And I'm planning on teaching you a lesson that you'll never forget." I opened the door she'd said to, and was only slightly disappointed to see that it was actually her bedroom. My palm itched to spank her again.

"Wrong about what?" She asked. I kicked the door shut and locked it before turning back to her bed. She squeaked when I unceremoniously dumped her onto it, and leaned over her, caging her in with my arms.

"I do own you Juniper Wild. I owned you the moment you walked into the hardware store that I was working at, and tried to make me believe that you really needed my help finding a hammer. I owned you the moment you opened those lips and let me kiss you behind the ice-cream shop that you pretended to sneak out and meet me at. And I owned you the moment you spread those pretty thighs and let me take you on the floor of that barn. I own you, pretty girl, and you own me too."

I kissed her, devoured her, drove my tongue down her throat and branded her mouth with mine. She thought she could lie and hide the truth about what was happening from me? She could try. I would suck it out of her very soul. Something had scared her. Something had made her close up in fear. But I was going to break down those barriers one delicious orgasm at a time. But first, she needed to be punished for lying to me. Again.

I pulled back and stood up to my full height, looking down at her on the bed, her honey blonde hair splayed out on the creamy bedspread, her eyes dark with lust. I took off my jacket and t-shirt, then slowly unzipped my jeans. She sat up on her elbows, her eyes tracking my movements. And when I was completely undressed, palming my erection in my hand, I came to stand directly in front of her.

"Are you ready for your punishment?"

She looked up at me and licked her lips. "I'm still not sure I need to be punished."

I leaned down and gripped her jaw. "You do. Remember, you asked for this. I told you to be careful what you wished for." Then I wound my fingers in her hair, pulling her into a sitting position and toward me. "Suck."

## 23

### JUNIPER

"Suck."

He growled the command at me, and part of me wanted to test his limits and resist. But the other part of me that had teased him back at the old Fuller barn, reveled in the fierceness. I flicked my tongue out, teasing along the head as I looked up at him with wide eyes. His fingers in my hair tightened, and I smirked. He might think he was in control at the moment, punishing me for not telling him who had spray painted the skull on my car, but I knew I held him in the palm of my hand. Literally. My hands cupped his balls as I swirled my tongue around his thick length, and when he growled out the command again, I inhaled as much of him down my throat as I possibly could.

"Fuuuuck, Juniper." He closed his eyes and tipped his head back in pure bliss. I pulled back, hollowing out my cheeks as I sucked, until my lips came off the tip of his cock with an audible *pop*. Then I did it again, setting the rhythm and pace as he watched me with hooded eyes. When I felt the salty taste of pre-cum on my tongue he pulled me back with a rough. "Enough!" And I batted my lashes at him.

"What's wrong, Cade? I thought you wanted me to suck?" I pouted coyly, then grinned.

"You're a fucking minx, pretty girl." He smirked down at me. "But you aren't getting off that easily. Are you ready to tell me about the skull?"

I glared at him. I'd genuinely been hoping the distraction would work, and he'd forget all about the morbid image spray-painted on my car.

He shook his head. "Fine, have it your way."

Before I had time to even think, he'd pulled me up and switched positions with him sitting on the bed where I had just been. Only this time I wasn't standing, I was bent over his knees with his hard erection pressing into my stomach, and my hands pinned behind my back. I gasped. "What the hell, Cade! What are you doing?"

"Punishing you." Somehow with his other hand, he managed to grab the top of my jeans and jerk them down over my hips and ass, exposing everything to the air and to his eyes. I squirmed. "You are *not* going to spank me! This is absolutely ridiculous. I don't have to tell you everything Cade Black."

"You're right" I felt his firm and calloused hand graze the globe of my cheek, stroking and massaging it almost lovingly. Heat traveled strait to my core and my eyes widened in surprised. No way in hell was I enjoying this. "You don't have to tell me everything. But I would highly encourage you that you do." He leaned down, his rich voice a dark purr in my ear. "And I am absolutely going to spank this pretty ass of yours as part of that encouragement." And then, I felt the sharp sting of his palm on my skin, and I yelped. Rapid-fire, three more smacks came, burning my poor ass cheek, then before the sting could give way to pain, his hand was massaging me again, soothing away the hurt. I felt his fingers dip between my cheeks to my pussy, teasing through the wetness I realized had been pooling there. "Mmm, wet for me? I thought you didn't like getting spanked." His teasing voice made me tense.

"I don't!" But even I didn't believe my own lie. Every touch sent little shocks of pleasure and pain through me. His fingers found my entrance and he teased my opening. I wiggled on his lap, searching for more.

"You're a terrible liar, pretty girl." More spanks came, this time on my other cheek, and I couldn't hide the moan that escaped. Just like before, his hand massaged my burning skin before dipping down to run through my wetness, dancing around my clit and opening, but never giving me what I wanted.

"Ready to tell me yet?" I bit my lip, refusing to speak. He paused for a half a moment and then repeated the same pattern. Three rapid-fire smacks against my ass before his fingers would dip and tease me. He pinched my clit and I nearly came undone, but he pulled back just before I got the release I was seeking.

"No, no cuming for you. Not until you promise to tell me what you know." I groaned. I was a puddle of goo on this man's lap, and didn't know if I could survive anymore. He eased his fingers partway into my pussy before pulling back out, giving me just a taste of what I wanted.

"Fine! Fine! I'll tell you. Please just stop. Or don't stop!" I gasped as he grazed against my clit again. "Oh God, please don't stop."

He chuckled and I was released, then carefully placed on my feet where he finished removing my clothes, allowing me a chance to catch my breath and collect my thoughts.

I closed my eyes and groaned when he dipped his head to my breast, drawing one nipple into his mouth and lavishing it with his tongue before moving on to the next. "If you want the truth you're going to have to stop distracting me." With a grin he bit down slightly and then pulled away.

"Fine, pretty girl, but make it fast or I might spank you again for keeping me waiting." The delicious promise in his voice had me melting all over again.

"The truth is, I don't know who painted that skull." When he growled a warning I shook my head."I'm telling you the truth. I don't know who did it, but I know what it means." I licked my lips nervously but he remained silent, waiting for me to continue.

"When I was a little girl, I found a book of photos in the attic. They were old, really, really old." I remembered the excitement I'd felt at discovering something that had seemed so magical at the time. "I showed my mother and we sat on her bed looking through them, trying to determine who they were and how they were related to our family."

Cade listened, a frown furrowing his brow as he

listened to me. "Eventually, we figured out that they must be photos from when the city was founded. Or at least, not long after that. And there were more that spanned generations. It was like looking through a history book. Only it was our family's history."

He pulled me closer to him, his hands running over my hips. "Speed it up, Juniper. What did you find?"

"I found a photo of a group of people, only it was different from the others. The people in this photo were all dressed up and standing in front of a fireplace, but I couldn't see their faces. They were all wearing masks." I shivered, remembering how my mother's smile had fallen, her entire body going still as I'd raised up the photo, pointing out the masks that had looked so funny to me at the time. I'd asked her if they were at a Halloween party and she'd just nodded, taking the photo from me and tucking it in the back of the album.

"All of the people in that photo were holding a piece of paper. It looked almost like an invitation. That skull was on it." I licked my lips suddenly nervous. Cade's eyes narrowed as he watched me.

"There's something else, isn't there?" His gaze was

full of suspicion, but his tone was encouraging me to continue.

"I can't be sure. It was so long ago and I was barely ten years old, but I remember turning the photo over and there was a list of names. Many of them were Wild's but there was one name that stuck out to me. D. Black." I saw the surprise in his eyes and the confusion. What was a Black doing with a group of Wilds? "There's more, D. Black was the only name crossed out on the list."

He stood up and kissed me suddenly, taking my breath away with the ferocity of it. I pulled back and searched his face, trying to figure out what he was thinking. "Cade, don't you understand? That picture scared my mother. It scared her enough that she refused to tell me what it meant or who it was. And now, someone is spray painting that skull on my stuff. First my garden shed, now my car. Someone has marked me and I don't know what it means." Fear bled into my voice and for the first time, I let it show just how worried I was. He cupped my face between my hands, his hazel eyes flashing.

"Someone has done this before?"

I nodded and he snarled, his eyes hardening, the scar on his face standing out in stark contrast to the golden tan of his skin. He kissed me again, then picked me up before placing me gently down on my bed and covering me with his body. Desire flared once more, and I raised my hips to grind against his hardness, desperately seeking to be closer to him.

I felt the thick head of his cock against my wet opening and I moaned, my nails digging into his hips in encouragement. I wanted to forget the skull, forget the photo, forget the worry and fear that had been swirling in my gut ever since I saw the first mark. He looked down at me, eyes dark with lust and something else. Something I wasn't sure I wanted to name yet. I closed my eyes but he paused and made a disapproving sound. "Oh no. Eyes on me, pretty girl. I don't give a shit about pictures, skulls or anything to do with the past. This is the now. This is us. Just you and me. And I'm not letting anything get in the way of that again."

And then he was filling me, stretching me, until he bottomed-out with a groan, before pulling back to do it all over again. He kept his eyes locked onto mine the entire time, demanding that I stay there in the moment with him. Pulling back he sat up, spreading my legs, his hips pistoning in and out, driving his cock over that delicious spot deep inside until I was a soaking mess.

"Spread your pussy, let's see how well you take

me, pretty girl." I moaned, the dirty words going straight to my clit and my hands slipped down, spreading my lips apart as he drove into me. My fingertips just grazed my clit and I arched off the bed, the orgasm sending waves of pleasure through me.

"That's it. Play with your cunt and come on my cock while I fuck you." He growled and my fingers found my overly sensitive bundle of nerves again, stroking and teasing through the wetness while he pounded into me. The orgasm built again, and I felt him harden even more, his hips losing control, and I cried out at the same time that I felt him bottom-out, spasming deep inside of me. Sparks danced behind my eyes, as the orgasm took my breath away and he collapsed on me, sweaty and breathing hard.

He rolled to the side, pulling me with him and tucking me into his chest before placing a soft kiss in my hair. "I'm sorry, I forgot a condom."

"It's fine." I murmured and yawned. "I'm on the pill."

"Good, because I plan to do that again." I smiled against his chest and closed my eyes, letting the bliss of post-orgasmic sex, lull me into sleep.

## 24

CADE

*I* slipped from the bed, the early afternoon sun pouring through her bedroom window, and went to the attached, master suite bathroom. It was softer, more feminine than I imagined it being, considering this was a master bedroom suite and Edmund Wild had been the main resident for so long. A picture in a gilded frame on the bathroom counter, made me realize who had originally occupied the room, as I stared at a woman who could have been Juniper's near-twin, if it weren't for some small differences. Blaire Wild had a slightly more-pointed jaw, and her skin tone was more porcelain compared to Juniper's gold-kissed glow. But it was clear that Blaire's genes were the most dominant, because everything else was almost the exact same. It made me wonder even more who Juniper's real father could be.

It also made me wonder: if Blaire had been pregnant before she married Edmund, why had she gotten married to him at all? Edmund Wild didn't strike me as the type of man to tolerate his wife carrying another man's child. Or choosing to take on the responsibility of raising her.

My gaze caught on something that glinted in the light from the bathroom windows, and I had to swallow back a feeling that I didn't want to acknowledge. A bracelet was on a tray on the counter. The kind of bracelet kids made from letters and beads, strung together on a cord and given as gifts. The kind of bracelet you threw away once it became too threadbare to wear anymore, and the letters were nearly unreadable, just like this one was. I picked it up, staring at it in amazement. She'd kept it all these years. A birthday gift I'd given her when I hadn't had enough money to buy her the things I'd wanted to. The things she'd deserved. *Pretty Girl* was spelled out in silver beads, capped with more beads of purple and pink glass. The nickname I'd given her since the first day she'd walked into the hardware store where I had clerked, and had stolen my breath away.

I clutched the bracelet and shoved it into the

pocket of my jeans. Fuck what Kage wanted. Juniper deserved to know the truth. We'd spent too long apart with lies and secrets between us, to begin again with more lies and more secrets. She'd been open and honest about the skull and the mysterious photo, even though I could see she hadn't wanted to share it with me. Not because she wanted to hide it but because she was scared.

Her fear had been a real and palatable thing, and I knew that the skulls and photo were somehow connected to what Kage was telling me I needed to protect her from. But before I could tell Juniper the truth about her parents and Edmund Wild's fake death, I needed answers. Why was my last name on the back of that photograph? Why was it crossed off?

I pulled out my phone and hit "dial". He picked up on the third ring.

"Someone painted a skull with a crown of flames on her car. Want to tell me what that's all about?"

He was silent and I looked at my phone, checking to see that we were still connected. "Start talking Kage, I need answers."

I heard a sigh. "This isn't a conversation we should be having over the phone."

I swore. "Fuck you. This is a conversation we should have had a long time ago apparently. You knew didn't you? You knew before you asked me to keep an eye on her that Edmund Wild was alive. And you knew about these marks and what they mean. When were you going to tell me?"

He snarled. "When the time was right. You think this is easy for me? You think I enjoyed waking up one day to realize I had a sister I never knew about, and she'd been working, living, breathing, right under my nose for the past five fucking years?"

I stilled. "Sister? Juniper is your sister?"

He swore and I could hear the sound of him pacing. After a few moments he came back on the line. "Yes, Juniper is my half-sister. We have the same father."

I didn't know what to say. But it added a layer of complexity to the situation, and now I questioned whether my plan to tell Juniper the truth was a good one, or not. This wasn't something she should be hearing from me.

"How did that happen?" Disbelief clouded my voice.

"Well, Cade..." Kage drawled with dark sarcasm. "...when two people like each other—" I cut him off. "You know what I mean, asshole. How did Juniper's mom and your dad even meet? Does this mean Edmund knows that she's not his daughter?"

"Those are questions I don't have answers to yet. And yeah, I'm pretty sure he'd have to of known about the affair. Listen, I wish I could tell you more but I can't right now. I have to run. I'll be in Wild in two days time and can answer more questions then, and I should hopefully have more answers."

My jaw clenched in frustration but I understood. "Fine. But I want answers when you get back. I don't like keeping this from her. And brother or not, she deserves to know the truth about her parents and Edmund Wild."

"You're right. She deserves to know, but I'd like to be the one to tell her about our dad. Please, do this for me." Kage never begged. For him to be pleading with me now, let me know just how important this was to him. I ran a hand down my face and nodded even though he couldn't see me.

"Yeah, I understand. You should be the one to tell her. But what about the skulls? She's scared and this isn't the first time it's happened either." I didn't say anything about my name being on the back of the creepy photograph.

"It's a mark. Back in the day, secret societies sprung up all over the place with almost cult-like fanaticism. People were fascinated with the occult and mysticism back then. And even though it was just a poor mountain city at first, Wild wasn't immune to it. They made pacts with each other and pledged allegiances in blood." His voice was dark and ominous. "If Juniper is finding the mark on her property I doubt it's an invitation to join. She's being warned."

"She found a photograph when she was a kid of a group of people in masks holding a piece of paper with that sign on it. Do you think they were the original members?" Was my family an original member? The question swirled around in my head.

His voice perked up. "She has a photograph?"

"She did. I don't know if she still does. It was probably fifteen years ago that she found it. Before her mother died." I glanced at the picture of Blaire on the counter and frowned. Had she known about the secret society? What had made her so afraid?

"Cade, listen to me, I need that photograph. I don't care what you have to do. Get it for me. I'll be in Wild in two days with more answers and we'll figure it out." Kage's voice bit out in a harsh demand.

"And what am I supposed to tell her? How am I supposed to get the photo from her without letting her know what's going on?"

He laughed. "You're Cade Black. You've taken down some of the most blood-thirsty and dangerous men I've ever seen, and did it without breaking a sweat. Are you afraid of one woman?"

"Hardly without breaking a sweat. Did you forget about the scar that asshole, Romanov, gave me? And this is different. You know how I feel about Juniper. I don't like keeping this from her." Especially now that we'd just reconnected, I finished silently.

"Yeah..." He deadpanned. "About that, we'll be discussing your intentions with my sister when I get there as well."

"She's been your sister for all of a week and now you're suddenly Mr. overprotective brother?" I snorted.

"I don't mess around when it comes to my family, Cade, you of all people, should know this." His voice was a dark promise and I tensed at the underlying threat there. Kage was ruthless on most days. But when it came to his family? His viciousness was legendary. There was no one he wouldn't cut through, betray, or destroy to protect them.

"I know. But know this, you can drop the 'bullshit brother' act right now. She doesn't know you. You aren't going to come bull dozing into her life and take over, Kage. She doesn't need to be a part of the world of death and destruction you revel in. Juniper stays out of it, do you understand?" I wasn't backing down. Kage may have been one of my closest and oldest friends, but I would fight to my last breath to protect Juniper from the dark depths of society that he dwelled in. Brother or not. He could go fuck himself.

He laughed, and the hair on the back of my neck stood up. "We'll see Cade. We shall see. I have to go. Remember, two days. Get the photograph and protect our girl." Then he hung up, and I was once again left staring at my phone, wishing I could reach through and punch the asshole.

"I have a brother?" The soft voice behind me cut straight to the gut, and I whirled around in surprise.

She was standing there, her hair a golden mess around her shoulders from our earlier activities, and the nap that had followed. But there was nothing sleepy or tired about the blue eyes that pierced me right to soul. Eyes that were full of the pain, hurt and shock of betrayal.

I took a step toward her. "Juniper, I don't know what you heard but..."

She interrupted me, tugging down my t-shirt that she'd thrown on over her naked body. "I heard everything." She frowned, looking away as if she was still trying to piece together what she'd just witnessed. "Or at least, I think I heard everything. I can't really be sure, especially since you just conspired to keep it a secret from me." She looked at me again and I swallowed, seeing for the first time the possible resemblance between her and Kage. A dark anger flashed in the depths of her blue eyes. Fuck. I was in trouble.

## 25

JUNIPER

My ears were ringing. I'd woken up starving from the lack of real food, other than coffee. Pain lanced through my head and I reached for the first article of clothing I could find, Cade's t-shirt, pulling it on. If I didn't get some food and medicine soon, the migraine would descend, and I'd be in bed the rest of the day, at least. My migraines had started just a couple of years ago, and I'd learned the tricks to control them over time. Make sure I ate and got plenty of sleep, limit the caffeine, and if I felt one coming on, head it off early with meds and rest.

Then I'd heard a low voice coming from my bathroom, and my name. Cade's voice. I walked toward the cracked bathroom door, with the intent to ask him about that breakfast he'd promised me, even though it was probably well-past lunch time now, when I'd heard words that had sent my thoughts into a spiral.

*"Fine. But I want answers when you get back. Brother or not, she deserves to know the truth about her parents and that Edmund Wild is alive."*

*Alive.* I'd stood, in stunned silence, as his words filtered through the door. I could only hear his half of the conversation, but what I did hear was enough for me to realize three things. I had a brother I didn't know about, Edmund Wild wasn't dead, and Cade had been hiding it from me.

No, not just hiding it from me. Working with someone to keep it from me. The man on the other end of the phone. My brother.

"How long?" I croaked out. My throat was raw from our earlier activities, and my voice was breaking from the emotions I was trying to choke back. "How long have you known?"

His face was a wall of stone. "About your brother? I just found out."

"About my dad, I mean," I had to pause before I could continue. "...he's alive?"

He took a step forward, reaching for me, but there was no remorse in his gaze. I stepped back, shaking my head. Sharp pain radiated behind my eyes. So much for trying to fend off the coming storm. "Don't come near me. Just tell me the truth."

He dropped his hands to his side. "Since last night."

"And when where you going to tell me? Oh wait. You weren't." I seethed, turning away and stalking back toward the bed. The bed where he'd tortured me with pleasure and pain, until I'd opened up about the skulls that had been haunting my dreams, ever since the first one showed up.

"Was this your plan all along, Cade? Was this payback for what I did to you?" I ripped his shirt off, suddenly not wanting any part of him touching my body, and I didn't care that I stood there fully naked in front of him. The room was spinning as if I was in the middle of a tornado, and I raged. Or maybe it was just me.

"You rigged the auction and made me the enemy of half the women in this city. You watched me. Tracked me. That's how you showed up at the bar that night." I turned around and began dragging out my clothes, angrily dressing myself. I felt like I was going to be sick.

Cade followed me into the room, leaning against

the door of the bathroom and crossed his arms. "And?"

I slammed a dresser drawer shut, and marched over to my bedroom door, opening it wide.

"And?! And, I thought we'd put the past behind us. I thought we'd moved on beyond petty bullshit like this. But apparently that's not the case. I should have listened to my father all those years ago. Wilds and Blacks don't belong together." I glared at him, not caring that he stood there with guilt and shame in his eyes. "Get out."

He watched me and then shook his head with a smirk that turned my furry into a raging inferno. "I don't think so, pretty girl. You're in danger and until you're safe, I'm not going anywhere." He picked his shirt up off the floor where I'd thrown it and pulled it over his head, muscles and abs flexing as he did so, and the fact that I noticed pissed me off even more. "What do you want for breakfast?" The casual way he asked the question made me want to claw his face.

Black spots danced before my eyes and I swayed slightly on my feet, but I didn't let go of the door handle. "The fuck you aren't. You're not responsible for me, Cade, no matter what bullshit idea you have that you own me. You can't own a person unless they allow you to. And guess what? I won't."

He stalked toward me and I didn't back away, holding my ground, even as it swayed under my feet. His fingers tipped my chin up, and the look in his eyes was dark, turbulent, and wholly unapologetic. "That's where you're wrong, Juniper Wild. Yes, I rigged the auction on purpose as revenge for what you did to me and yes, I was there at the bar that night because I was told to watch over you." He moved in closer until my back was pressed fully against my bedroom door, and I had no room to move around him. "And yeah, I agreed to keep the fact that Edmund was alive from you," he cocked his head, hazel eyes staring into mine,"...for the time being." The pad of his thumb traced my bottom lip."But you've never not been mine."

His head lowered, lips brushing against mine in a whisper of a kiss, before he moved away and headed down the hall toward the kitchen, as if he owned the place. I watched him, dumbstruck.

Waves of pain radiated through my skull, reminding me that no matter what happened, if I didn't get food and meds I'd be in no shape to continue a conversation, or anything else for that matter.

I followed him down the hall and, brushing past him as I reached the kitchen, went right for the pantry and a box of pop-tarts. Just as I was about to open the silver foiled packet, it was snatched out of my hands. "You aren't going to eat that garbage."

I whipped around, glaring. "I have to eat now in order to take my meds or I'm going to be in bed for the next two days trying not to puke my guts out."

He frowned at me. "What do you mean medicine? What's wrong?"

I moaned, half in pain and half in frustration, and dropped my elbows to the kitchen island counter, placing my head in my hands to hide my eyes from the light that was streaming in from the large windows. "Cade please, it's already bad, just give me some bread or something so I can take my medicine."

Without a word he turned around and began pulling open cabinet doors, placing ingredients on the counter and then next thing I knew the smell of something amazing hit my senses. I sniffed, raising my head, just the slightest, to see him standing over the stove, flipping something in a pan like he was a five-star chef. I blinked, unsure if my blurry vision was deceiving me. Cade cooked? A minute later a plate slid in front of me, and he was guiding me onto a stool.

I eyed the toasted concoction of bread, cheese and meat suspiciously. "Is this a grilled cheese?" He'd cut the sandwich in half, and as I picked up one half, the cheese dripped from it, making my mouth water.

He smirked. "It's a Croque Monsieur. Basically a French grilled cheese." He set a glass of orange juice down next to my plate. "Where are your meds?"

I pointed to a small cabinet next to the sink and took a bite into the sandwich, moaning as the explosion of gruyère cheese, ham and butter melted into my mouth. This was fucking delicious. My medicine was set down next to me, and then he stood there, arms crossed and a scowl on his face as I chewed.

"What's your problem, Cade?" After I'd had enough bites to know that I wasn't going to throw up once the medicine hit my system, I opened the bottle cap and took out two pills, swallowing them down with the orange juice.

He frowned, his scowl deepening. "I don't know what you mean."

"Well, you're standing there glaring at me like I've done something to piss you off when I'm the one who should be pissed off at you." I finished off the first half of my sandwich and started on the other.

"I'm not mad. And you aren't mad at me either." The frown lifted slightly, but he still glared at me, watching every bite that I took.

I sighed and set the rest of the sandwich down.

Hopefully the meds would kick in sooner rather than later, but the food had already gone a long way to help. Maybe I'd just been hangry earlier, and in shock, but he was right, I wasn't as mad as I'd thought I was.

"I'm not angry with you, but I am upset. I have a brother? My father is alive?" I shook my head, looking away from him for a moment. "You knew about it and planned not to tell me. And maybe I can see why. If I had a brother that didn't know about me I'd want to be the one to tell him too. But my dad? How did you plan to keep that from me? And why?"

He moved closer to where I was sitting and nudged my plate. "Eat. When you're feeling better we can talk."

I glared at him. "My dad is alive somehow and I have a brother I've never met. I think we can talk *now.*"

We stared each other down for a moment before he nodded. "Fine, but not until you've finished eating."

"You talk. I'll eat." I picked my sandwich up and took a bite, then stared at him pointedly. He frowned again, but then pulled up another stool to sit at the counter across from me.

"I don't know a lot, your..." He paused as if the word was as unfamiliar to him as it was to me"...brother hasn't filled me in on a ton of the details. But yes, you have a brother and yes Edmund Wild is alive."

Hearing the words from him directly was just as shocking as when I'd accidentally overheard him the first time. "I don't understand, how? How did my dad have another kid and why, if he's really alive, hasn't he come back? Where is he?"

Cade waited until I took another bite, pointedly staring at my Croque Monsieur pointedly, before answering. "Your dad didn't have another kid. Your mom had you. And why Edmund hasn't come back is still a mystery, but your brother believes that because you aren't biologically his heir, you are in danger."

Another shock I wasn't prepared for. My mother had an affair? And I was the product of that affair? I tried to wrap my head around the information I was receiving. "Da- Edmund, faked his death to get me to come back for something. That's what you're saying?" Cade nodded, staying silent.

"And the skulls? What do they have to do with anything?" My mothers fear-filled eyes flashed in my mind. Cade shook his head, sighing.

"We aren't sure. Your brother is looking into it. He'd like me to bring him the photograph you mentioned, if you still have it." I nodded, staring down at the rest of the sandwich on my plate, suddenly not hungry. The pain in my head had lessoned to a dull throbbing, but the pain in my heart was another story. I had a brother and apparently a father I didn't know about. And the man I'd thought *was* my father, the man I'd grieved for no matter how much he'd hurt me in the past, was alive. Alive, and a threat to me now. Lost in my thoughts and memories, I didn't pay attention to the front door opening or hear the footsteps coming into the kitchen.

"Hey, what's this thing that was in our mailbox?" Dean's sneakers squeaked on the hardwood floor, as he rounded the corner and came to a surprised halt.

"What the hell are you doing here?" His curt voice made me whip around.

"Dean! Language!" But Dean ignored me, his eyes locked onto Cade, his jaw set stubbornly. Cade arched a brow, cocking his head slightly.

"I'm talking to your sister, like you asked me to."

I blinked, I'd completely forgotten that Dean had asked Cade to talk to me about his school suspension. Then I winced. I'd also completely forgotten about the meeting I was supposed to schedule with the principal. Some guardian I was.

"Oh." Deans face softened and he shifted on his feet, looking awkwardly between me and Cade. My heart clenched again. Maybe I wouldn't be Dean's guardian for much longer. If my dad was really alive would he come for Dean too? I bit my lip. Would Dean want him to? And how did I tell him?

"Dean, I..." The words died on my tongue when I saw what he was holding in his hand. "What's that?"

He held up the paper and the envelope it came, walking over to the counter to show me. "I don't know, but it's super creepy."

I took it from him, my hands shaking. On the creamy, thick paper, was only one image. A skull in red with a flaming circle around its head like a crown. On the bottom in gorgeous calligraphy font, was a date and an address.

I looked at Cade. "I think I just got an invitation."

## EPILOGUE

Flames flickered in the firelight, logs crackling and snapping, a mesmerizing dance for the eyes.

"Mr. Wild. You have a visitor."

"Send him in."

The door to his office opened, but he didn't turn around to greet the man. You don't acknowledge those who are beneath you.

"Mr. Wild. You sent for me?"

The flames danced, oranges and reds blending, moving, swirling. He could almost make out shapes and figures. Faces grinning and smiling. No, not faces. Skulls. Or maybe it was just his eyes playing tricks on him.

"Mr. Wild?"

He blinked. "How useful do you believe you are to the organization, Mr. Myer?"

The man shifted uneasily behind him. "Well, sir, I believe I've been very useful since I joined."

"Hmm..." The flames danced, the silhouette of a woman now. Moving, sensual, reaching for him. A laughing skull raced across the cracking log. He shifted in his leather chair.

"You had one job to do Mr. Myer. Did you do it?"

He could hear the man swallow nervously. Could hear the rapid beating of his heart. Or maybe it was the snapping of wood as another log cracked and split. The woman's silhouette turned away from him, reaching for something else, another figure emerging from embers. A man. He snarled.

"No, Mr. Wild, not yet. But I am working on a plan."

The figures met in the center of the fireplace, twirling, embracing, their passion soaring as the flames leapt higher. His fingers flexed leaving deep grooves in the leather of his chair.

"It's too late for a plan, Mr. Myer. You had your chance and you failed."

"No, it's not too late, sir. I know Juniper better than anyone, we dated for months. I know I can get to her-" He held his finger up and the man went silent.

"That won't be necessary Jax." He didn't look at him when he raised his gun and fired a single shot. He just watched as the figures that danced in the flames dissolved into laughing skulls once more. "My daughter is already home."

The End....for now.

AFTERWORD

Ok, who needs a bandaid? A hug? Maybe you want to write me a love letter telling me how much you loved it and can't wait for the next one? I'm kidding about the bandaid and hug part, but I do love to hear from readers. Please be sure to email me authoranneroman@gmail.com

And please, reviews are so helpful to authors, even if you hated it although I hope you didn't and in that case I will probably be the one who needs a hug. So leave that review and be sure to join my mailing list at www.anneromanauthor.com to find out when Cade & Juniper's story will be continuing. Because I might like to drop you off the edge of a cliff from time to time, but I'll NEVER leave you hanging. Xoxo- Anne

## AFTERWORD

*Did you enjoy the book? Consider purchasing the entire e-book to own. Kindle Unlimited is a fantastic resource for readers and authors alike but only permits the author to earn royalties off of one read-through. Your support helps authors like me continue to write and do what we love. Thank you so much for reading!*

ACKNOWLEDGMENTS

I can't leave without acknowledging the people that made this book happen.

To my kids and family. Thank you for letting me write when I said I needed to get words in and for being so patient with me. I love you and I'm so thankful for you.

To my Muffin's. You know who you are. Thank you for always being ready to garden, read, laugh, and encourage me in everything. I love you all so much.

To my author friends and mentors, Amelia and Debbie, I couldn't do it without you. Thank you so much for all your guidance and advice.

To my beta readers and my beautiful editor Mandy. You guys really made this book come together. Thank you for being patient with me through all the changes and updates and rewrites. You're brilliant and I'm so thankful for you.

And to my readers. I hope I spark even just a

moment of joy with every book I write in someone, and if that someone is you, I'm so thankful for you. Xoxo- Anne

ABOUT THE AUTHOR

Anne Roman is the author of suspenseful, 'edge of your seat' romance. She loves to write exciting twists and turns that leave her readers begging for more. When not writing you can find Anne playing Uber driver to one of her four children, hanging out with her hunky husband, or catering to two very spoiled cats and one spoiled dog. Want to get to know her? Join her Facebook group here:

Anne Roman- Romance on the Edge

Made in the USA
Las Vegas, NV
16 November 2023